Guardian Angel

Undercover Series Book 2

Ruchi Singh

Books By Ruchi Singh

English

Novels

Romantic Suspense

The Bodyguard - Undercover Series # 1

Guardian Angel - Undercover Series # 2

Romance

Jugnu - The Firefly

Take 2 - Small Town Girl #1

My Love, A Liar - Small Town Girl #2

Short Stories

Women From Mars : Series Shorts

Temptation

Spark

Hearts & Hots - Series Shorts

Head Over Heels

You and Only You

Silent Love

A Promise is a Promise

हिंदी
एहसास - मेहरा ख़ानदान # १
काली नज़र - मेहरा ख़ानदान # २
लफ़ंगा - मेहरा ख़ानदान # ३ (जल्द ही ऐमज़ॉन पर)
टेक २ - नज़रों का खेल

The Man

Security expert Nikhil Mahajan is in mortal danger. Gravely injured and unable to see, he is in the midst of hostile strangers in an unknown place. Any hope of survival is fast fading away.

The Angel

Should an innocent man be left to die just because he had been in the wrong place at the wrong time? Someone has to intervene.

Guardian Angel

Undercover Series

Book 2

By

Ruchi Singh

To

my daughter
Malvika

PROLOGUE

'**Poor** girl, an orphan now,' people whispered, thinking she couldn't hear them.

Orphan. The word echoed in her mind as she watched her father—no, what remained of her father—draped in the Tricolor and taken to the cremation ground. She knew what state the body had been found in, what had been done to him. Even though people didn't talk about it in front of her, she had heard the horrified whispers and shocked mutterings. She was not an imbecile; she knew the harsh reality of her world, her state.

Not a single tear came to her eyes. She couldn't cry twice for the same loss, could she? From the day her father had been kidnapped, she had known she would not see him alive. She had mourned for both of them— her mother and father—at the same time.

She gave a small start as the gun salute in honor of her father started. Orphan. The word echoed with every report of the guns. He was gone. Gone like her mother, who had been gunned down when their vehicle had been attacked and her father dragged away.

Why had she gone on the high-school trip? she lamented again. Why had she insisted? Thrown all kinds of tantrums that had forced her mother to finally give in? She should have been with them on that day. She should have died with her mother. God was punishing her for being selfish. She had wanted to have fun with her friends and look what came after fun—sheer torture.

Orphan. She closed her eyes.

She felt a heavy hand on her shoulder and opened her eyes to look up at her father's best friend and mentor.

"Come with me, *beta*."

***

"Do you think this will work?" She stood at the departure gate—uncertain of her future—gazing at the electronic display board that showed her flight to Canada was on schedule.

"Of course, it will. Time is the biggest healer and studying the right subjects will take your mind off the—"

"Yes, I know, I know, Uncle Krishnan, not another lecture, please…" She rolled her eyes and tried to smile. It had been two months since the funeral. Her tears had dried, but the ache in her heart hadn't dulled.

"Remember everything I have told you. When the time is right, I'll call you."

"And you'll remember your promise?"

"Yes, of course."

"I'm really serious."

"Yes, I have no doubt." Her father's mentor, and now her legal guardian, raised his hand in farewell.

***

CHAPTER ONE

Hurried movement could be seen in a dilapidated hut hidden by the high pine trees of the Tral forest. The dusty road leading to it was full of potholes and fallen tree trunks. A battered, mud-splattered Mahindra SUV was parked in the haphazardly cleared vegetation near the hut. A small generator hummed in rhythm with the resident pigeons, who had accepted the generator as part of their habitat.

Near dusk, another black vehicle, in a shade better condition than the other, drove into the forest area with its headlights switched off and stopped near the old vehicle. A clean-shaven, bespectacled man, over six feet tall, clad in *khakhi* trousers and a white shirt, alighted from the front seat of the vehicle. The driver remained in the vehicle with the engine running.

"Salaam, Shehzaad *bhai*," Rehaan said, coming out of the hut to welcome him. "Some refreshments, *kahwah*, Shehz…" Rehaan trailed off as he encountered the cold, grey eyes of his cousin. Shehzaad was the group's third-in-command, feared next only to his uncle Altaf Muhammad. Rumor had it that Shehzaad had butchered his commanding officer when the last mission had failed because of his boss's womanizing ways, and had been promoted to take his place.

"Altaf *chacha* will be coming?" Rehaan asked. His mother had been pestering him for news of his uncle. The last they had seen him was at Id, several years ago, and that visit too had been for an hour only. Money was scarce again. They could barely get by on Rehaan's father's pension.

"What are the arrangements?" Shehzaad asked gruffly, ignoring Rehaan's question.

"*Ji bhai*, everything is set. We are ready whenever you say."

"He is at home?"

"*Ji, bhai.*"

"Why not here?"

"Who'll take care of him here?"

"Hmm… What did the doctor say?"

"He has done what he could, now the bastard has to heal before we can begin."

"How many days?"

"Two weeks."

"What if we start right now?"

"We won't have enough time with him. There are a few third-degree burns too, his body might not be able to take it at the moment."

"Hmm…" Shehzaad scratched his arm. "Bring him a week from now. Just make sure he doesn't die before we get all the information out of him."

"*Ji.*" Rehaan hesitated, then blurted out, "One more thing that you should know, *bhai.*"

Seeing Shehzaad's eyebrows narrow into a single line above the pair of steely grey eyes, Rehaan's heart sank to the pit of his stomach.

"Seth is searching for him like a madman. His pictures are all over the media."

"How come? I thought everyone presumed he was dead. Hadn't you planted a body and his things in the blast debris?"

"Yes, but they did a DNA test of the remains and apparently got the results yesterday."

"Yesterday, huh?" Shehzaad smirked. "Don't fret. It has been four days since the blast. He can never be traced now. But caution *khala* and your fiancée to take the utmost care."

***

Ayesha's eyes snapped open, her senses on alert. She glanced at the empty cot beside her. *Khala,* her aunt, must have got up to go to the bathroom, but it was not that which had woken her. She heard the clinking of the chain on the backyard door and looked at the window. It was still dark outside. The rusted chrome and neon hands of the old table-clock showed it was three a.m. A loud thwack came from the corridor. Someone scolded someone, albeit in hushed whispers. What was happening?

She threw the blanket aside and fingered her favorite blue-stone ring, unsure whether to go outside. There might be other men. It happened quite often that strange, unknown men visited the house, and *khala* never failed to reprimand her when her curiosity got the better of propriety. Still, Ayesha donned her *phiran*, wrapped the *dupatta* around her head and face so that only her eyes and nose were visible, and cautiously opened the door. The rooms were arranged around a covered corridor running around the central courtyard so that all the doors were visible to anyone stepping out of any room.

Her heart leaped to her throat when she saw the door to the basement stairs open. Experience told her to remain inside the room and come out only when she was called, which she invariably would be, since the visitors always needed refreshments. She was never allowed to go into the basement when the meetings took place though. It was always Rehaan who carried the food she prepared downstairs. Yes, it was prudent to remain in her room for now. But as usual, it was her curiosity that won over prudence. Quietly, she stepped outside and stood behind a pillar from where she could see the stairs leading to the basement.

Someone whispered in the stairwell. Then *khala* muttered some instructions. It was then Ayesha noticed that the wooden cot laid out in the corridor was missing and the three chairs from the basement were arranged haphazardly in its place. Had they brought someone who was sick? From the shuffling and footsteps, Ayesha could make out there were two more men apart from Rehaan, whom she would be seeing after almost a week.

She tiptoed toward the stairs. Nothing was visible since the stairs curved down into the small basement room. She heard her name mentioned by Rehaan, and *khala* disagreeing to something he said. Ayesha crept down three steps, ready to run back to her room at any moment.

"There is no other way," Rehaan was saying. "You won't be able to run up and down so many times in a day. And I won't have time. Moreover, she can read the prescription and administer the medicines."

"I don't see a problem, he's totally harmless in this condition," a man said.

"Shall I wake her now?" *khala* asked.

"No need. She'll get up in two hours' time, that'll be good enough," the man said.

Ayesha took one more step down, then realized with a jolt that they were moving toward the stairs! She scrambled back up the stairs and ran noiselessly to her room. She was closing the door to the room when they appeared on the threshold of the stairs. Taking off the *dupatta* and the *phiran* in one fluid motion, she lay under the blanket, trying to calm her breaths.

Khala came inside after a few minutes and climbed into her bed. Soon, her gentle snores filled the air, and Ayesha allowed herself a quiet sigh of relief.

Ayesha spent the couple of hours before the daybreak lying awake and wondering what lay in store for her? Or to be precise, who lay in the basement?

*****

Ayesha listened without paying much attention as *khala* droned on and on, repeating pretty much every instruction again and again. Ayesha had been told there was a sick man in the dusty basement room and she was supposed to nurse him because *khala* couldn't climb up and down the stairs, and Ayesha was the only one who had a rudimentary knowledge of English to read the doctor's prescription and understand the right dosage.

Who was he, she wondered? Another one of Rehaan's friends who had landed in trouble? Either way, it was yet another hateful addition to her back-breaking burden of household chores.

"Are you even paying attention to me?" *khala* yelled.

Ayesha bobbed her head and picked up the prescription and the medicine packet doctor *saab* had given to Rehaan.

She looked at the man lying on the narrow cot. He wasn't sick. He was pretty battered. His left leg and arm were in a cast and his entire right side was swathed with bandages. It seemed he was still wearing his own clothes, though portions had been cut off for easy access to his injuries, and she could see the burnt, frayed edges where the embers must have hit him. Rehaan had said he was injured in a fire. Who was he kidding? Being in the valley, she knew the man had been in a bomb blast.

"What's wrong with his eyes? There is nothing in the prescription about the eyes."

"You are not to open his eye bandages at all. We can't have him looking at you, sweetheart." Rehaan drawled, running his fingers up and down her arm discreetly. Then, he grinned and took off his hand. "Don't you get it, Ayesha? We can't take the risk of him recognizing any of us."

Ayesha nodded, pretending to be immersed in reading the prescription. So, the man was not a friend. Who, then? There was no name on the paper. The man had suffered several second-degree burns and a few third-degree ones on the leg. Most of the burns were on the right side of his face, and on his right leg. His torso and right arm bore no burns but were covered in bruises of all sizes. Perhaps he had been wearing a jacket or a coat which had saved that part of his body from the blast.

She was given strict instructions by Rehaan to keep the burns and the wounds clean, and the man hydrated.

And she had also been instructed by *khala* to keep her gab shut around him and about him. As if!

This wasn't the first time the basement room had been used to hide a prisoner. Rehaan had been tasked by Shehzaad to raise the funds for the holy war and for spreading unrest in the area. And kidnappings for ransom were one of the ways the group raised money.

From the name of the famous brand on his trousers, the injured man certainly seemed reasonably wealthy. Was this another kidnapping? Something told her, though, that this prisoner was different. For one, he was not a local, like the other kidnapping victims had been. Also, she had heard no mention of money from Rehaan or anyone else. Why, then, had he been brought here, that too in such a state?

***

CHAPTER TWO

The intense burning sensation penetrated Nikhil's brain before he could even open his eyes—then, the realization struck. He couldn't open his eyes! They were bandaged. He thrashed at the sheet covering him to tear off the bandage on his eyes and a fresh wave of panic rode on his senses. He couldn't even move his hands or legs. They seemed to be bound. What had happened? What was wrong with him? What was wrong with his eyes? He tried to recall what had happened to him but his memory failed to oblige. Where was he? He struggled again against his bonds and heaved with the lack of oxygen.

"Bhagwan deenai hammat… theek gazzak…"

A melodious, feminine lilt reached his consciousness, even as his right hand was held in a soft, but firm, grip. The panic receded even though he couldn't comprehend the language, but his heart continued to hammer in his chest.

"Doctor?... Nurse?"

The woman remained silent. Perhaps she was just an attendant.

"What's wrong with me? What has happened?" he croaked, his throat parched and aching. "Why are my eyes bandaged? Is there something wrong with my eyes? I… I… where's the doctor?" Uncertainty led to fear again, then panic. He thrashed again, gasping for air. "I want to talk to someone… I want to see the doctor—"

"No, no," the woman whispered in English, then continued in the native language, trying to soothe him.

"Please call Vikram," he blurted. His subconscious had suddenly thrown up the name of the one person who would never leave his side in this condition.

Vikram! Every sliver of memory rushed whirled like it were in a kaleidoscope, bringing on another round of blind panic. Vikram! Vikram's life was in danger! There was an assassin on the loose, bent on killing him. And then, there was the lead! A man who claimed to know where the unknown assailant was getting his arms from. Nikhil had gone to the Kamathipura dance bar to meet the informant. But then, what had happened? His mind drew a blank. All he knew was that he shouldn't be here! Who would be taking care of Vikram's security in his absence? He had to be with Vikram.

He fought down the panic and forced himself to concentrate. His injuries. How had he got them? Thinking about that brought forth a hazy recollection of a blast, of being thrown back against the stained glass of the bar. A bomb blast? In Mumbai, yes. But, where was he now? A hospital room, perhaps? How many days had passed? Were his parents somewhere around in the hospital?

"My father—"

The attendant seemed to have trouble understanding since she continued to tend to his wounds, which seemed to him to cover every inch of his body. He switched to Hindi. "Can you please call someone from my family, I want to talk to them."

The woman continued to change the dressing as if she hadn't heard him.

Fuck, what's wrong with the lady? His pragmatic mind told him to get a grip on himself. He forced himself to clear his mind and take deep breaths. His legs and arms ached and felt stiff, they must be in a cast. Yes, that must be the reason he wasn't able to move them. As he calmed down, he inhaled the musky aroma of burning wood and ginger. Was the hospital canteen nearby?

He winced as the woman began to undo the bandage on his thigh. For fuck's sake, how many were there? His body tensed at the burning sensation every time she touched and cleaned a wound, then she applied something that brought instant relief.

"Call the doctor," he snapped weakly. "…the doctor."

"No, no." The woman held his arm as he pulled at the sheet near his fingers and tried to soothe him again.

Oh God, did she know only one word?

"Please." Uttering even a few words was an effort. How had he become so weak? He curled his palms into fists; there was no IV needle on them. His vision-impaired senses summarized that there was no humming of medical instruments around, as should have existed in a hospital room. The temperature was cold as if the room was air-conditioned, but the antiseptic smell associated with hospitals was absent.

Where was he? Was he at home? What was the day?

As she worked on his torso he began to slide into deep slumber. He fought against the stupor he was sinking into. He wanted some answers. How was she inducing sleep without drugs? Nowhere during her ministrations had he sensed a needle pricking his body.

From a far distance he heard a man snap, and the girl answer in hushed reverence. The voices faded away as Nikhil drifted off into comfortable oblivion.

***

Ayesha glanced at the unconscious, troubled man. He looked worried even in his sleep. She wanted to assure him that his injuries were not fatal but Rehaan had warned her that under no circumstance was she supposed to converse with him. Picking up the tray on which she had arranged his medicines and lotions she turned to go, but a groan stopped her on her tracks.

She looked back.

He was still but breathing erratically. The unkempt locks of hair on his forehead and the four-day stubble on his fair skin made him look all the more pale and vulnerable. The burn on his cheek was deep and would leave an ugly scar. The faint lines around his mouth told her he hadn't led an easy life. How had he fallen in Rehaan and Shehzaad's clutches? Why was he here? What did they plan to do with him?

She knew that Rehaan indulged in activities she was not privy to; still, she knew much more than *khala* and Rehaan thought she did, thanks to Rehaan's tendency to brag. He would disappear for days, then would come back disheveled and hungry, but pepped up. In those circumstances, he usually let on more than he realized. A couple of times she had gone so far as to show her disapproval, but he had reacted violently and thenceforth she had kept her own counsel. Not that she had any hold over him with *khala* pouring her destructive venom of *jihad* in his ears day in and day out.

Ever since she had come to this big house after her parents' death, *khala* had offloaded every household chore on her. The family had had a name in the village a long time back, but after *khala's* husband's death and the unrest everything had gone downhill. Now, even though they still lived in the largest house in the village, their living standards had come down significantly as they were forced to subsist on *khala's* pension and Rehaan's dubious earnings.

Her patient stirred, bringing her out of her musings. He turned his head this way and that, muttering a word again and again. She stepped closer to the cot and leaned. 'Vikram.' He was calling for Vikram again. Who was this Vikram? She had no means to check. She'd have to go to the neighbor's house for news. Or maybe she could borrow Asma's phone for a while.

"Ph…shsh."

Ayesha turned around to find Rehaan urgently beckoning to her from the stairs. She followed him up the stairs, through the courtyard to the backyard.

"Why were you leaning on him?" he demanded, scowling, once they reached the trees surrounding their home.

"He was saying something that I was trying to hear."

"What was he saying?"

"He was repeating 'Vikram' again and again. Who is he, Rehaan? And who is Vikram?"

"No one. Just keep your mouth shut. You are not supposed to speak about this to anyone. Not even your stupid friends. Especially not Asma or Shabnam."

"I won't say anything to anyone. But please, Rehaan. Tell me at least."

"This is ultra-secret. A lot depends on me and you for this mission. You are playing a very important role in our war."

"What if he dies here?"

"Don't be fanciful. He is not on his deathbed. He'll recover and, in a few days, we'll take him from here."

"Where? Who is he?"

"Believe me, Ayesha, you are safer not knowing anything about him."

"Why are we—"

"You shouldn't ask so many questions," he snapped.

She bit her lip and stared at the pine tree behind him. Rehaan was getting exasperated and she reined in the urge to probe further. Instead, she allowed a pretty pout on her face, and Rehaan instantly regretted his outburst.

"Ayesha *jaan*, don't worry your pretty head with all this."

"Will Altaf *chacha* be coming for Shabnam's engagement?"

Rehaan smiled fondly. "His program is never known to anyone. Why are you so eager to meet him anyway?"

"*Khala* keeps talking about his work in Azaad Kashmir, and how grand and important he is, so I just wanted to see him. After all, he's your *chacha* and I've never met him."

"Yes, of course. He's a great man. Has kept the Indian army on its toes in and around Kulgam." Then, he smiled. "But why are we talking about all this? Let's talk about *us*… I rarely get you to myself…" He trailed a finger down her cheek, gently tucked a stray tendril of her hair behind her ear and gazed into her eyes.

"I think the old man is watching, he just turned toward the lake." She looked away from Rehaan's intense eyes to the Chinar trees and the lake beyond, as he caressed her lips with his thumb. The old man living near the lake was indeed looking at them. She knew he wouldn't be able to make out much with his cataract-ridden eyes, but still, it was unnerving when Rehaan stood so close.

"Ignore him. He's senile and deaf." With a finger on her chin, he tried to turn her face back to himself. "Are you angry with me?"

She shook her head.

"Rehaan!" *khala* shouted from the kitchen. Her eagle eyes never missed anything. Though Ayesha and Rehaan were officially engaged, *khala* kept a tight leash over them.

"*Ammi*, for the love of *Allah*, I'm not doing anything," Rehaan shouted back, then whispered, "Listen, love, let me do the thinking, you just follow, *phir ham sabko jannat nasseb hogi, jannat.*"

Ayesha kept her mouth shut as always, though she suspected it was hell, not heaven, they would all go to.

***

CHAPTER THREE

Ayesha came down the next morning to find her patient thrashing on the cot, trying to be free of his bonds, fists clenching and releasing. He was delirious and mumbling something. Then, suddenly, he became still. So still that for a second she thought he was dead. Slowly she stepped toward the cot and placed a finger under his nose to check for breath. He twitched making her lurch back in fear and her head banged against the door.

'Allah, what a fright!' She giggled with one hand on her heart and other rubbing her head.

"*Yah, Allah! Kya hua?*" *khala* called from the upper floor.

Unwilling to disturb her patient, Ayesha ran up the stairs and appraised her that the man was running a high temperature.

"Then do whatever you have to do," *khala* said and washed her hands off the matter as usual.

The wounds might have inflamed, Ayesha surmised. Thanks to her regular trips to the local doctor because of *khala's* chronic ailments, Ayesha knew most of the regular medicines and the care involved. She took a clean piece of cloth and a bowl of water and went down the stairs.

***

Nikhil woke up to the same musty smell of burning wood and something spicy this time. Something like cardamom or cinnamon, he wasn't sure. His body ached—the familiar agony, every time he woke up. How many times had he woken up like this, and in how many days? He didn't have any idea. Time had lost its relevance with his eyes closed under the bandage.

The nurse or the attendant was by his side every time he had woken up. She had checked on his wounds, mopped his brows with a cool cloth, and fed him with the help of straws. Everything—medicines, water, milk, sometimes a salty lentil broth—was patiently coaxed down his throat. He had a bizarre notion that she had even prayed for his recovery.

That day, however, no one was by his side when he woke up.

After calling for the nurse repeatedly, he tried to locate the bedside bell. It was an effort to lift his arms. His right arm was bandaged from elbow to palm, but there was no choice, as the left was completely immobile. He lifted the arm up, and a sharp pain radiated through the inner side, but he persisted. With the limited movement, he could not find the iron rails of the hospital bed. Groaning, he stretched some more. There was nothing above his head as far as he could reach. He straightened his arm painfully and touched the bed below the sheets. He was lying on a wooden cot with a thin mattress.

His growing doubt that he was not in a hospital was turning into a frightening reality.

All this while, as he had drifted in and out of consciousness, he had consoled himself with the thought that he was being cared for in a hospital and his family and well-wishers were around him—perhaps at his bedside or, if he was in the ICU, outside the room.

No wonder he hadn't heard a familiar voice for the past… past how many… how many what? Hours? Days? Weeks?

And what about Vikram? Was he safe? Who was guarding him now? Nikhil had immense faith in the chain of command he had set up in case of his absence. Esha, Jay, and Uday were more than capable of handling any situation thrown at them. But would Esha be able to cope while operating undercover?

And if he was not in a hospital, then he had added more work for them—that of searching for him. He was sure they would be looking for him though he didn't know since when?

What an extremely foolish step he had taken going alone. Overconfident of his ability and anonymity, he had stepped into unknown territory without backup, without even informing anyone, that too in a hired taxi. And he was now paying the price. All his identification documents were in the taxi he had kept engaged during the meeting. The meeting to which his informer had never showed up.

Somewhere to his left, a wooden slat creaked and clothes rustled. Somebody was coming. He pretended to be asleep. The woman entered and didn't pay any attention to him. By the sounds, he understood she was cleaning the room.

She methodically finished her work and left, ignoring him altogether.

The bandage on his eyes was a bit too tight and had begun to itch. Nikhil moved his right arm and gently tried to bend it at the elbow. He gasped in pain and let the arm fall back on the cot. He took a few deep breaths. Some kind of muscular tear had brought about that spasm. Clenching his teeth against the agony, he tried again. This time he managed, with effort, to bring his hand to his face.

He gingerly inserted his right finger in the crevice formed by his nose, careful not to touch any wound. There was no pain in the outer area as he moved his finger under the bandage. Encouraged, he pushed the finger up and swiped his fingers over the eyelids. There was nothing—no pain, no cotton swab, no ointment—his right eye was absolutely fine. The only discomfort was in his throbbing arm caused by the movement.

After a few minutes of rest, he repeated the same process for the left eye and got the same results. There was nothing wrong with his eyes! Excited, he loosened the bandage with his hand and fluttered his eyelids. Gingerly he opened one of the eyes. He could see the color of his skin… the tip of his nose… the brick wall in front.

The floorboard creaked again. He straightened and pretended to be resigned to his situation, unwilling to let on that he knew he could see. The woman entered the room. Clothes rustled. She kept something down and the door creaked shut.

He peeked again. He was in a room roughly eight-by-eight feet in size. The walls were not even plastered; there went the last hope that this place was a hospital or at least a clinic of some sort. There was only one door and no window. A fire sputtered and crackled in the *angithi,* kept near the door, out of his reach. Bastards.

Where was he? What if he removed his eye bandage? Bandage? No, blindfold. And with that term, his situation hit him square in the face. He was not a patient, but a prisoner!

He took deep breaths and tried to clear his mind. He'd have to think things through before doing anything. At least his vision was intact. He knew the status of his arms—on the left something was broken. The right was a little better, with only the lower arm bandaged. He moved his toes. Nothing wrong there though two of the right toes were bandaged and throbbed as he moved them. He couldn't move his left leg at all, but his right knee and leg seemed okay, except for the burns.

He pretended to sleep when the stairs creaked again. The woman entered. From the sweet, spicy whiff of food she brought with her, it seemed it was meal-time. Lunch or dinner, he couldn't fathom. He waited for her to begin dressing his wounds, but could sense no activity for a few seconds. What was she doing? Had she seen him moving? Was the blindfold loose?

He relaxed when she sighed and began on his ankles.

"Where am I?" he asked. His voice came out hoarse. He cleared his throat.

Her hands stilled at his voice, then resumed the task, but he didn't get an answer.

"Who are you?"

He heard bottles and tubes being opened and tinkered with.

"Talk to me, damn it!" he snapped.

"Sh…sh…"

"Do not shut me up!" he shouted. "I need answers!"

"Have you gone mad!" she finally hissed in Hindi.

"You can speak Hindi!"

"Yes, and please do not talk," she whispered.

"Why not? I'm going to shout if you don't answer my questions," he said in Hindi.

She didn't answer.

"Hello! Anyone here!" Nikhil shouted, his voice no louder than a croak. He began to cough, triggering an avalanche of pain all over his body.

"Keep quiet, just keep quiet. They are going to take you from here if they know you are fit and fine, which you are not!"

"I'm going to pieces not knowing anything! Where am I, ma'am? And who are you?" Nikhil lowered his voice.

"Just think that I'm your shield. Till the time you are under my care, it's okay."

"What happens after that? Please, I request you, do not talk in riddles." *God, where had he landed!*

"I don't know anything else."

"Tell me whatever you can. I can take it."

He was again subjected to silent treatment.

"So?" he prodded.

She expelled a long breath but didn't say more.

"Is this a hospital? A clinic? Where am I? And who are you? Some kind of a healer, or a quack?"

He heard her suck in her breath in disapproval as she jabbed the straw in his mouth a little too forcefully making him spurt and cough. Good, she could be riled. Maybe he could make her lower her guard and give him some information. Or maybe he'd have to resort to sweet-talk.

"I'm sorry, I didn't mean to insult you," he said after finishing the milk she had forced him to drink. "How long have I been here?"

"Four days."

Four fucking days!

"At least tell me... where am I?" he mumbled.

The question was answered with silence.

"Am I in Mumbai?"

"No."

"Delhi?"

"No."

"Jammu?"

Silence.

"Kashmir?"

She took a deep breath.

"Oh, is there a ration on questions too?" So they were in Kashmir, he had guessed the language correctly. But he had no recollection whatsoever of the journey from Mumbai to this godforsaken place.

Someone shouted, an old woman. The girl answered in the affirmative in their native language. They were very cautious not to take names. What did they want from him? Was this the gang after Vikram's life?

"Hey, listen!"

No response.

"Your medicines," she said after a while, nudging a pill into his mouth.

He dutifully opened his mouth and, after taking the pill, he allowed her to insert the straw in his mouth again. To keep her in good humor, he drank the lightly salted broth and swallowed the other pills too.

"Please, may I know the extent of my injuries?"

She remained silent, arranging the coarse blanket over him. So the subject of his health was taboo too. He changed tack.

"Hey, doc. My name is Nikhil. My friend in Mumbai… Vikram Seth, can you get me some news about him? Please. It must be all over the media, you might get some information from the newspapers or TV."

Silence.

He sighed. "I need to go to the bathroom."

She didn't say anything but left the room immediately.

He heard two people entering the room ten minutes later, including the girl. Someone taped his mouth shut. He struggled, or tried to struggle, against the hands which were pulling him up to a standing position.

"Bathroom *jaana hai ki nahin*?" a man hissed.

Nikhil then realized he was being taken upstairs. He had to lean heavily on the man as his legs refused to support him. He was taken up the stairs and across an open courtyard. Winter sun-rays warmed his arms and neck. The man guided him through the entire excursion since he could use only one hand, then brought him back to the room.

To his concern, he found himself completely drained of energy. He longed to lay back on the cot. A trip to the bathroom had tired him out? Only four days had done this to him? Four days without proper medical care—he qualified his statement. Four days was what the woman had said. Was it more than that? How could he trust her?

The woman touched the straw to his lips. He drank the salty, yet tasty, broth.

The fog of sleep began to cloud his mind. The woman must have given him a sleeping pill or put something in the concoction. Fighting the lethargy spreading all over, he tried to think logically but soon lost the battle.

***

Ayesha feared she had said more than required in exasperation. But she couldn't help it, he could have brought *khala* down, or worse, Rehaan. He sounded desperate, and she was so tired. She had not slept properly in the last three days with Rehaan hovering around her, twiddling his thumbs, fretting about what would happen if the man died. It was a huge relief to see him awake and talking.

So relieved was she with his recovery that she had had an overwhelming urge to put him at ease and reassure him that everything would be alright. Sympathy had her blurting out things when she shouldn't even have spoken to him in the first place. But he looked so helpless—injured, blindfolded and bound like an animal. Lying in the same position for so many days… and nights.

He didn't know but she knew there was nothing wrong with his left arm. Only his shoulder had been dislocated, which had been set right. They had bound the arm to a thin plank so that he wouldn't be able to remove the blindfold.

For the past three days, delirious, he had continuously muttered his friend's name, but once or twice he had called out for his mother too. Her heart had twisted in her chest at that.

He was a grown man but vulnerable as a child in this condition.

The least she could do was find out about his friend.

It had to be on Asma's phone. Borrowing Rehaan's phone was a complete no-no. Even if she deleted the history, he had ways of finding out about her searches. She had learned about his fascination with her and her interests the hard way.

In the afternoon she sought out Asma and borrowed her phone. The moment she typed Vikram Seth and hit enter, the screen was filled with photos and news about the assassination attempts on Seth, the bomb blast in Mumbai, the kidnapping of Esha Sinha, Seth's assistant, and the death of the assassin in the subsequent encounter.

Someone had been trying to kill Vikram Seth, a renowned industrialist. There had been two attempts on his life. Nikhil Mahajan was his security-in-charge and actively involved in the investigations. He was presumed dead in a bomb blast in Kamathipura, a red-light area in Mumbai, but later it turned out that he was missing, not dead. His watch and wallet had been found in the debris of the blast, but DNA reports had revealed that his body was not at the site. There was a massive hunt going on for him and a huge reward for anyone who gave any information about his whereabouts.

The award was so huge that Rehaan would normally have salivated over it. So what was he waiting for? Vikram Seth was a multimillionaire, and Nikhil Mahajan was his right-hand man. In subsequent articles, it seemed he was more than that—more like a brother. Was this the reason Rehaan was keeping him alive, to get more money? Was he waiting for the reward money to rise?

As she sifted through the news items, her glance fell on the person behind Vikram Seth in one of the shots. Was he Nikhil Mahajan, the man she had been tending to for the past four days? She zoomed into the photo. The man was wearing a dark blue shirt, tan colored trousers, and sunshades.

She zoomed more.

At first, she could find no resemblance to the person lying in the basement. But as she studied the photo, feature by feature, it became clear that it was indeed the same man. She couldn't believe what an accident could do to a human being. He looked so different on the screen—so virile and thriving.

Quickly going through the news about Seth, she was able to find a couple of more clicks with Mahajan in them. Though he always remained in the background, his presence could not be ignored. Taller than his friend, and more muscular, he was so full of life that even in the stills he appeared to be in motion.

The man lying in the basement was just a shadow of the one in the photographs. He looked so helpless, more so with the blindfold.

Whatever was happening was not right. Her conscience bothered her every minute of the day. Should she at least tell Mahajan there was nothing wrong with his eyes and give an excuse that the blindfold was just a precaution against harsh light for a few days?

No, no…what if Rehaan came to know? She had been cautioned that the prisoner shouldn't be able to recognize anyone or anything associated with the house, else there would be a price to pay. A blood price.

She rotated the ring on her finger, a subconscious act she resorted to whenever her mind was in turmoil, unable to come to a satisfactory solution.

"Are you coming to the market?" Asma asked when she handed over the mobile.

"Let me ask *khala*." It would be a good respite; she had missed going last Friday too.

***

It was only after lunch that Ayesha could summon the courage to seek *khala's* permission for a trip to the Friday market. The usual lecture and taunts began the moment she asked the dreaded question.

"*Allah!* This girl! Always thinks of her own fancies! What will happen if he calls?" she waved her hands toward the basement stairs.

"He is sleeping and won't wake up for another three hours. But it's fine… I won't go… it's only that Asma asked," Ayesha said unemotionally. She had learned not to push hard. Asking for something matter-of-factly usually worked better with the old matriarch.

"Go then, if she is going. What can I say if you have already made the program? I hate to say anything about the dead, especially my own sister, but didn't your mother teach you anything? You should have asked me first."

"I didn't agree to anything, *khala,*" Ayesha protested, but *khala* was on a roll.

"But I know you… always looking for some excuse or the other to go to Asma's house or to the market. Anything to avoid work. It is only for the sake of my poor departed sister that I have taken you in."

Ayesha sighed, her eyes downcast. She really wanted to go.

"Oh… ho… go. Take the purple *burqah*. The other one has a hole. What will the neighbors think? Remember your place and behave in a way that does not bring shame upon your dead parents. Otherwise, there is no dearth of good girls for my Rehaan. If he marries elsewhere, you'll be out on the streets."

Ayesha picked up her *burqah* and went out with Asma and her younger brother. She ignored the old man who nodded at them as they went past him toward the main market.

***

In one of the offices in the Secretariat, New Delhi, a man, in his late fifties, sat studying the various reports lying on his desk. He looked up as his secretary entered the room and handed him a fax.

"Do you want it to be translated?" she asked.

He shook his head, and the woman retreated closing the door softly behind her. The man looked at the message and translated. His German was as good as his native language Tamil. Then he painstakingly decoded the message:

'They have brought an injured man to the house. Nikhil Mahajan. Don't know why.'

He sat staring at the message for a long time, then took out his lighter and torched the message as well as the paper on which he had decoded it.

***

CHAPTER FOUR

In the evening the man came again when Nikhil woke up.

"Where am I?" Nikhil asked him. Without answering he taped Nikhil's mouth shut and took him to the pathetic toilet up the rickety stairs again, even when Nikhil didn't want to go. The cold draught of air told him that the door was open. In any case, Nikhil was too constipated and too much in pain to bother.

"Where have you brought me? What do you want from me?" Nikhil asked again, once they were back in the room and the tape was taken off.

The man ignored him and laid him back on the filthy cot.

"Who are you?"

No response.

Nikhil heard him go up the stairs.

He heard the tinkle of bells. Were they anklets today, or bangles? His Florence Nightingale was coming down. This time he was determined not to ingest anything she gave him. It seemed they wanted to keep him sedated and confused all the time. Liquids are good for you, she had said once. He'd be damned if he drank any broth mixed with sleeping pills she gave him tonight.

"Any news of Vikram?" he asked the moment she entered.

She began the ritual of poking the straw between his lips. He sipped a few drops. It was water so he drank all of it.

"About Vikram—"

"He is fine, his assassin has been killed in an encounter," she answered.

A wave of relief swept through him and he sent out a silent prayer to God Almighty. But the next second doubts assailed him. Should he believe her? Why would she lie? Maybe to keep him calm. *'What the fuck!'*

"Are you sure?" he asked.

"Yes, I saw it on the news. It's all over the media."

She sounded… well honest. In any case, he had to get out of this mess first to help Vikram. "Can you please tell your boss I was just investigating my case and have nothing to do with anything else?"

She inserted the straw again and he spat it out.

"Listen, I was about to meet an arms dealer in that bar, who might have sold something to Vikram's assassin. That was the reason I was there and nothing more."

She tried to insert the straw again, he tightened his lips.

She expelled her breath loudly in exasperation. "Look," she hissed. "I can't help you. I'm only here because they are short of people and can't cook. Moreover, who listens to a woman? We are just born to serve. Please have this soup so that my work is over and I can rest."

"What is it? A sleeping potion? If so, I'm not having it. I'm done ingesting sleeping pills."

"You'll heal better if you sleep through the night… and day," she said softly.

"Trying to fatten the pig before the slaughter?"

She didn't insist further and left without feeding him.

In the dim light in the room and with his limited view, he studied the room. There was nothing much to see, of course, and he soon began to get restless. The discomfort of lying in the same position began to assert itself with a vengeance. His skin itched. He wanted to turn to his side and his stomach growled. She was right. He was better off sleeping away the hours. Lying there unable to move with nothing to see or do, nothing to distract him from his discomfort, was torturous. Something bit him on the lower back. He was sure it was a bed bug. He twisted and squirmed so that the sucker would get off his skin but nothing helped.

Then he heard her.

She came near him and touched the straw to his mouth. This time he drank without protest.

Ayesha sat next to the cot and watched him drift off to sleep. Something about him tugged at her heart. Was it because he was completely dependent on her? Despite her pretended exasperation, his little act of defiance earlier had somehow filled her own heart with hope. But it hadn't taken him long to realize how hopeless his position was.

The bombing had broken his body, and Shehzaad would break his soul.

***

A strange yearning kept Ayesha restless the whole night. She had done whatever she could, but was that enough? She had made him comfortable under the circumstances with the resources she had at her disposal. Hiding from *khala*, she had fed him lamb broth too. But the question remained, was that enough?

Earlier only sympathy had driven her, but now…

Earlier he was a stranger but after seeing his photographs and his world, she wanted to know more about him. Did he have a family? Parents? A wife? They must be looking for him. She kept mentally going over the conversation she had had with him, but other than Vikram and his mother, he had taken no other name.

His vitality in the photos and his helplessness down in the basement overlapped again and again in her mind, not letting her sleep.

After tossing and turning for more than an hour, she tiptoed down the stairs. He was sleeping with his face turned away. From her vantage point, she could see his profile—the chiseled jaw and the sharp nose. What would be the color of his eyes? So far she had not been able to figure that out from the photos she had found. In the pictures, he mostly had his sunglasses on. In the video clip she had seen, he walked like a person in control of his destiny.

Would she be able to see him walk? Ever?

He turned his face and muttered something. She took a step forward when she heard him groan.

'Esha!'

Ayesha stopped and frowned. Who could that be? A sliver of green envy pierced her heart. After a while, she turned around and stormed up the stairs. Sleepless, she tossed and turned in bed again. Who was Esha? It was only after she had decided to borrow Asma's phone once again in the morning that she managed to drift off into a fitful sleep.

***

Nikhil woke up to hear wood crackling somewhere to his left. After a couple of minutes of waiting and listening, he lifted his head and tried to peek through the blindfold. Pale light from the low-wattage bulb bathed the room yellow.

His back had begun to ache, and he wanted to turn to his side. Then he heard her come down. He straightened his arm and turned his head toward the door. Time to figure out an escape plan.

"Hey, doc. Good morning." Nikhil feigned a cheerful facade. "Or should I say good evening? I have no idea. I've lost all sense of day and time."

She sighed, but said, "It's ten in the morning."

"I wonder why you guys have not bound my mouth, 24-by-7," Nikhil asked.

"The voice won't carry," she replied in a resigned tone.

"Then why were you worried the other day?"

"Only people in this house can hear, that too if the door is open."

He sighed. "What do you guys want from me?"

She sighed too.

"Can you turn me to my side?" he asked.

After a few seconds, she held his right hand, put a hand on his back and tried to help him. He clenched his teeth against the pain, but a moan still escaped him when he put his weight on his side.

She stopped.

"I don't think I can at the moment," he said dejectedly.

She was disappointed too, it seemed.

"I'll bring a pillow," she said and ran up the stairs before he could say anything. Nikhil couldn't understand her. She was such a simpleton. Making him comfortable when she knew he was a prisoner.

She rushed down, her bangles tinkling, and arranged the pillow behind his back.

"Thank you," he said.

She picked up the straw.

"You smell quite nice, doc," he said. Following the sound of her feet, he turned his head a bit toward her and smiled.

Ayesha's heart skipped a beat. The smile had transformed him. For once she was glad that he had the blindfold on and could not see her blush. As it was she blushed easily and had been feeling hot from the time he had asked her to turn him. She had never felt like that for Rehaan, who was no less handsome.

But why was she lusting after a man who already had someone waiting for him? A man like him would definitely have a wife or a girlfriend. She shouldn't feel anything for him or be jealous of someone who had nothing to do with her.

She wasn't jealous! She was just curious. Yes, she was just curious about the life of the rich and happening, like one was about film stars and cricketers. Yes, that's the reason she had searched for Esha today on Google, but her curiosity was not quenched. She had been able to find

Esha's photograph in a couple of places with Seth, but none with Nikhil.

After searching for half an hour entering all permutations and combinations of the names, she hadn't found anything personal, except that Esha was an office assistant to Seth and was wounded when Seth was shot at after an event. She had left Seth's employment immediately after the life-threatening incident.

None of which answered the one question that was tormenting Ayesha—why had Nikhil called out *her* name?

***

Nikhil was already awake when she tinkled into the room the next time. He didn't move. Normally he followed her as she worked around him. Let her sweat a bit thinking he had died. He could make out she was arranging the food and medicine on a recess made in the wall which served as a table.

"I know you are awake!" she said.

Hearing her amusement, Nikhil grinned. "How did you know?"

"Your plastered foot twitched when I came down."

"It's probably attracted to you."

Silence. He had embarrassed her, he thought. She was, after all, a sheltered, small-town girl. "Ah doc, don't give me that silent treatment. You are my window to the outside world. How can you remain silent? Tell me what should I call you? TV or Google?"

She went about her work without engaging with him again.

"Or shall I call you Roshni? You are the only ray of sunshine in my life. Or maybe Sunshine. Yes, Sunshine has a nice ring to it…"

He knew she wouldn't respond easily, but it was good to talk to someone even if the conversation was one-sided. If he was going to die soon, he'd be damned if he died of boredom.

"So Sunshine, how is the weather today? Is it snowing or is it sunny and bright?"

In answer, she ripped the bandage on his ankle.

"Aah…" He winced and smiled. "Oh, it's raining. Great, thanks for an answer." He smiled and winced, alternatively, as she changed his dressing. "Tell me something—" he began when the dressing was over.

"Water," she touched the straw to his lips.

"Do you use a different straw each time?"

She was provoked into snapping, "Hygiene is the least important thing you should be worried about at the moment."

"Will worry help my cause?"

She didn't say anything.

"I wonder what's the color of your eyes," he babbled with the straw still in his mouth.

"What's happening!" a man shouted.

In shocked reaction, she yanked the straw from his mouth. The water dribbled down the corner of his mouth as the utensil hit the ground.

"You are talking to him!" the man barked, now near the bed.

Then he heard a thwack. The girl gasped.

"What the hell!" Nikhil shouted. The man had slapped her!

There was a scuffle around the bed as the man continued to scold her in their native language. Nikhil couldn't understand a word. The girl grunted again and the bells in her ensemble jingled in protest. He heard her being dragged up the stairs.

"Wait… no!" Nikhil panted with anger, guilt, and helplessness, his limbs in agony as he struggled to rise. Then, there was silence in the room. He lay back on the cot praying she would be okay. Who was the man, anyway? Her brother? Or her husband?

After what seemed like an eternity, he heard her come in again. The depth of relief he felt at her return surprised him.

"Are you okay?" he asked.

She didn't answer. Of course, she wouldn't.

"I'm sorry," he said, softly, when she touched the straw again to his lips. Then, he opened his mouth and drank dutifully. She had changed the drink and given him a different kind of soup. It was delicious.

***

CHAPTER FIVE

Ayesha lightly touched her cheekbone, the pain radiated to her ear. In the rusted dressing mirror in her room, she examined the red-blue bruise and cursed Rehaan. For good measure, she cursed the man in the basement as well.

How dared he flirt with her when he had a girlfriend or a wife back home? How could he behave like that with her when he hadn't even seen her? Did he think she was an easy girl? And how could he behave like that when he was in such a dangerous situation? She was, after all, a member of the enemy camp. And yet, even in the condition he was in, he had tried to get up, to protect her!

She stomped out to the trees in the backyard after dinner. Everything was the same—peaceful and silent, totally in contrast with the turmoil in her heart. The full moonlight played on the surface of the lake and the old man sat smoking his *hukkah* with his back to the house.

She heard Rehaan cross the backyard and stop behind her.

"I'm sorry, *jaan*," he said.

She didn't say anything as her hands fisted around her ring. Let him wallow in guilt. She turned her head at an angle so that he could see the bruise.

"Ayesha… I lost control." He came around to face her. "I'm really sorry."

"You should have taped his mouth," she pouted.

"Then how we'll feed him, silly?" He touched his thumb to her lower lip.

"I don't know. You tell me. Is it my fault that he keeps asking for some Vikram?" she said.

"Just don't reply to anything he says."

"But I'm also human!" She blinked to make him guiltier.

"No, you are my doll."

"Please be serious. What are we going to do with him once he is able to sit? Who is this Vikram anyway? And who is this man? What is it to us if he lives or dies?"

"You shouldn't bother yourself with all this, Ayesha. This stuff is for men, not for delicate girls like you."

"I want to share in your successes, Rehaan. Will I not be proud to know your part in the holy war?"

He smiled. "Yes, of course. I'm playing an important part, and so are you. That man, well, he knows something which we want." He paused and, for a moment she thought he would say more, but he changed his mind. "It's enough for you to know that much. Now no more talking, okay." He tucked her hair behind her ear, then closed his eyes in frustration as *khala* called her name. "Here comes your keeper. Go and rest, love. You look tired."

She smiled letting the matter go, too tired to be angry. Also, he would hover around her if she didn't relent to his cajoling. Glancing across the lake, she noticed that the old man had retired for the night. Throwing a last look at Rehaan, she went inside.

***

"What do they want from me, Sunshine? Do you have any idea? Money?" he asked the next time she came down not giving her any respite. "Or are they going to torture me?"

The straw fell from her hands and her heart thudded painfully.

"Do you guys really hate Hindus?" he asked. "I doubt that. There must be many Hindus out here. I know not everyone has left. How are they able to live here? Are they your friends?"

She closed her eyes for a moment and remained silent.

"Don't you think you all will be better off if you do not rebel against your own country? India is progressive. Everyone will be happy and—"

"Keep quiet, just keep quiet," she snapped, not bothering to whisper.

His right hand twitched as if to touch her in apology. "I'm sorry I upset you." He waited for a while, then added. "I won't bother you again."

Tears appeared in her eyes. She blinked them away. After that, he stuck to his words letting her complete her chores in silence.

***

Ayesha ran to the tap in the courtyard and splashed water over her face. It still didn't help to control the trembling which had started from the time he had uttered the word 'torture'. Why was he raking up these subjects? And with her, of all people? What did he know about her? Nothing. She wished he had never come into her life. To take her mind off things, she went to find Asma.

She came back from the Asma's house to find *khala* packing.

"Pack your suitcase. We are going for Shabnam's engagement."

"But that's four days away!"

"Yes, we have to go and help them with the preparations." *Khala* had been preparing for her brother's daughter's wedding with unbridled enthusiasm. So much so that even Ayesha had been given a new outfit and bangles.

"What about him?" Ayesha asked gesturing toward the stairs.

"You don't have to bother about him anymore," *khala* said pulling out a bag from under the cot. "Aren't you happy? You are free from the extra chores."

"Yes… yes…" Ayesha said, looking toward the locked basement door.

"Close the kitchen too and pack the leftovers for Asma's family."

Ayesha nodded, spotting Rehaan going to the backyard with his phone. Rotating the ring on her finger, she stepped into the kitchen as *khala* continued to bellow last-minute instructions. The small kitchen window high up on the wall was a good place to satisfy her curiosity. Unknown to him she had heard many a conversation from there, which had given her a clear picture about Rehaan and his crusade. She stood up on the big tin box, used to store the grains and reached the opening.

"We can house any number of people…" Rehaan was saying, "…only three? Should not be a problem at all. There will be no one to cook though, but I can make arrangements. No, no. No problem… yes… of course."

There was a pause for a few seconds then he spoke again.

"Electricity? Yes, load shedding happens. Mostly at nights. Once or twice a week. Yes… yes… no, we don't have a generator. No, there is no power plug in the basement. Yes… okay."

After a few moments, he cursed under his breath. Curses which made her ears turn red. Then he kicked the wall and shouted, "*Ammi*!"

Ayesha climbed down the box and began to tidy the kitchen.

"Where's *ammi*? What are you doing?" Rehaan asked entering the kitchen.

"Packing the leftovers."

"Is there some food?"

"Yes. Mutton stew and lots of rice. *Khala* said we can give to Asma's family."

"No need. Just leave it here." He patted the wooden table just outside the kitchen.

"But, *khala* said—"

"Never mind what she said," he snapped. "I'm saying just leave it here."

"Aren't you coming with us?"

"No."

"Why?"

"Why do you ask so many questions?" he shouted, then stormed out of the house.

Khala and Ayesha left the village on the next bus. Shabnam's village was just fourteen kilometers away by road. Ayesha couldn't understand the urgency. They could have easily taken the morning bus.

***

The man in the plush office looked at the fax his secretary had placed on his desk. After decoding, it read:

'The house is vacated for the next five days, except the prisoner and the nephew. I think NM is innocent.'

The last line bothered him. Agents were supposed to give facts, not opinions. This couldn't be ignored. He picked up the phone and made a call.

***

CHAPTER SIX

Nikhil woke up to find himself tied on a hard, flat surface with the blindfold still in place missing the familiar warm ambience of the room. The cold seeping into his bones indicated he didn't have any clothes on except for his underwear. He tried to lift his right arm, but couldn't move it too. His arms and legs were tied with what seemed like nylon ropes. This realization raised his terror and confusion to new heights. His labored breaths accelerated, as he struggled to free his limbs.

"He's awake," someone muttered in Hindi then switched to the native language which got on his nerves.

A needle poked his left arm and his body relaxed, but this time he didn't drift to unconsciousness. His mind got disassociated with his body. He couldn't even move his head, but the anxiety left his body. He tried to segregate the various sounds around him. A man scuffled near his head, to his left. Someone else pulled a stool near the bed, to his right. Slowly he found himself smiling without any reason. What kind of drugs had they loaded in him?

The person to his right cleared his throat and spoke in English, "Mr. Nikhil Mahajan, we know who you are, and we also know why you were in that bar in Kamathipura. Now what we want to know from you is this—who told you the day and time of our meeting?"

Nikhil frowned, trying to follow the trail of the question, then grinned, unable to control his muscles and answer.

"What have you given him?" his interrogator barked after a moment.

"Amobarbital, the truth serum," the man on his left said.

"How much?"

This time the answer was in their language. Truth serum? What kind of truth did they want from him? His life was an open book. Everything confused him, yet everything made him smile. He tried to question them, but his tongue refused to obey.

The men kept arguing around him and suddenly the blindfold was off. His eyes cringed and didn't open under the harsh light. Someone forced his eyelid up. He heard a smattering of words: 'dilated', 'dosage', 'half an hour'. Then, they left the room.

The strong light from the naked bulb hanging from the roof made it impossible for him to open his eyes, still, he tried. The lure of eyesight after days of being almost blind made him force them open. His eyes began to water, but he managed to survey his surroundings.

He was in the same room minus the furniture, lying on a plywood plank placed on the bare cot. Holes were cut into the plywood to tie his limbs with nylon ropes. His left leg was still in a cast. The burns all over his body were still bandaged, but his left arm was without the cast. Wasn't there something wrong with it? He wasn't able to move it earlier. Everything was so confusing.

A gun-toting man in *khakhi* attire entered the room. The first thing that Nikhil saw was the emblem of a hawk on his cargo pants. The logo of the bird glowed in the shadows of the single light bulb swinging lightly from the ceiling.

"Hello, Mr. Mahajan." He sat on a stool near him.

Nikhil blinked under the high-wattage bulb, unable to see the man's face. Fear still failed to kick-in and he felt like smiling at the man again.

"Did you remember the evening at Kamathipura?"

Nikhil nodded.

"Why did you go there?"

"To… meet someone." He smiled, finding it humorous to string words together.

"Who?"

"An… an informer." He blinked in slow motion.

At his answer, someone moved near his head and the man leaned toward him in interest.

"Who was that informer?"

"An arms dealer," Nikhil knit his brows, trying to remember the lead. "One… one who I think was supplying arms… to the person who shot at Vikram."

"Who was that arms dealer? What was his name?"

"I don't know."

"Name, Mahajan, name?"

"I got a tip and was called to that bar."

"You are lying."

"No. Why do you want to know?" Curiosity made him blurt out the question and he realized that he was once again gaining control over his tongue.

"Mr. Mahajan, I'll explain to you only once. Here, I'm the one asking questions. Who told you about our meeting there?"

"I don't know about any other meeting."

"You are lying."

"I was there for my own investigations. I work at Seth Industries in the security department." The urge to grin and laugh was slowly leaving him.

"That's a nice undercover setup. We know Jayaram Sharma, aka Jay, runs that department. For the last time who told you about us, Mr. Mahajan? Or things will turn nasty."

There was absolute silence except the humming of some machine that sounded like a generator.

"I have absolutely no idea what you're talking about." Nikhil heard scuffling near the foot of the bed. Confusion and anxiety replaced the light, funny feeling. The effect of the drug was leaving him. A needle pricked his arm again. The man on his left mumbled something and his interrogator cursed. Nikhil felt the same kind of floating sensation, but this time he slowly drifted off to sleep. The voice of the man cursing at the top of his lungs faded away into the cold night.

The hawk in the emblem flew and danced in the yellow light.

***

Nikhil panted for air. He was drowning. His hands strained against the nylon ropes. A few seconds later he realized that they had thrown a bucket of water over him. As the water receded his panic was replaced with another kind of fear.

Men hovered over him, and he felt the scrape of a razor blade on his chest. They shaved his hair at some six to seven places all over the body, nicking the skin in haste. His heart hammered like an aircraft engine as they taped cold electrodes to the shaved areas.

The man in *khakhi* hovered over them. Two men crouched in the corner over a device, whispering softly. They were not going to kill him, Nikhil assured himself. Not after all the pains they had taken to keep him alive. But death would be preferable to the torture he had imagined over the past one week. Maybe he should say something just to get rid of the pain they were about to subject to him.

After a while, the faceless man held up a device up in his hand which had a red lever. "Do you know what this is?" The man tapped the lever. "If I press this, you will wish that you had never been born."

Nikhil pursed his lips in answer.

"Now listen to me carefully. Give me the truth and nothing will happen to you. One wrong answer, and you'll be sorry."

Nikhil looked in the general direction of the man without masking his loathing this time.

"Which organization are you working for?"

"Seth Industries."

The man pressed the lever. The shock was instant and beyond endurance. Nikhil closed his eyes and clamped his mouth trying to ride out the pain, unwilling to give them the satisfaction of hearing him scream, but he couldn't. The piercing, blood-curdling sound that emerged from his mouth startled him as much as the man on the other side who staggered back.

The interrogator lifted his finger and waited for Nikhil to get his breath back. Sweat poured down Nikhil's temple and soaked into his hair at the temple.

"I have all the time in the world, Mahajan. Everything's up to you. You tell me the truth and you can go back home."

"You bet," Nikhil panted, his voice hoarse.

The man pressed the lever again.

Nikhil lost all sense of time as the man kept asking the question for which he didn't have an answer. Or he didn't have the answer the man wanted. The agony was unbearable after every word he uttered. He was sure he was going to die every time the man cursed and pressed the lever. Survival took over as the man questioned him again.

"Where do you work?"

"IB?" The word came out as croak through his dry throat.

"A few more seconds of this and you will die, Mahajan. But… all this can end if you give me what I want."

Nikhil heaved without opening his eyes. What was the right answer? Wasn't the IB looking at internal terrorist situations?

"Are you listening to me, Mahajan?" the man hissed, his breath fanning his forehead. "Are you getting what I'm saying?"

Nikhil blinked his eyes and nodded. The bone on his plastered leg and the skin where the nylon ropes bound him, had begun to throb.

The man pressed the cursed lever again. Nikhil screamed again. The man lifted the lever immediately. The pain subsided but the aftermath had him panting and sweating profusely. He no longer felt the cold. His whole body was on fire.

"Who are you working for?"

"Army," he said and hoped it was the right answer.

"You are a very bad liar, Mahajan," the man said in a low tone and then something swished on his left and he heard glass shattering. Nikhil was too much in pain and tired to even be startled by the sudden volume and harshness of the tone.

"Do you think we all are fools out here?" his interrogator shouted. "Just admit who you are," he continued in an even tone, "and give me the name of the person who gave you the address and time on that day in Mumbai. You'll go scot-free, I promise."

"Hah…" Nikhil smirked, tiredly.

A second later he screamed as searing agony shot through every nerve of his body.

"Which organization are you working for?" the man asked once Nikhil got his breath back.

"RAW," Nikhil rasped, willing to say anything by then to make the pain stop.

The answer seemed to satisfy them.

"Who was the man? The name?"

"Irfan," Nikhil lied again taking the first Muslim name which came to his mind, hoping there was no one amongst them named Irfan.

"Irfan, who's Irfan?"

"I don't know. I know him by this name only," Nikhil said, not knowing whether the man was buying it or not.

The man pressed the lever again.

***

"*Bhai*, I think he's not the one we are looking for. It seems he doesn't know anything." Though Rehaan didn't show it, the blood-curdling screams were getting to him and he wanted it to end.

"What do you mean he's not the one?" the man barked, hands fisted. "Of course, he's the one and he'll have to tell the name of the defector amongst us."

Rehaan took a step back at the vehemence of his boss. "But we have tried everything in our capacity and there is no way he could be lying even after all this."

"You are still a softy, cousin. No, we haven't tried everything. Enough of these new-fangled ways. Tomorrow, we will go back to the good old way of interrogation. Everything will come out when we chop off his fingers one by one."

***

CHAPTER SEVEN

'**It** will be over soon.' Nikhil chanted the words like a talisman, gasping for breath and licking his dry lips. He was drenched in sweat, the skin under the electrodes was burned due to the heat, and his wrists and ankles had chafed raw under the nylon ropes. How many hours had passed? He didn't have any idea.

They had asked the same question again and again and, not knowing which answer would satisfy them, he had given the same answers again and again. The interrogation and the torture had gone on and on till... he didn't know when he had passed out. The room was dark now, and he was alone. But he knew they would be back, and that he would not survive the next round of interrogation. Oddly, the thought brought only relief; he wanted this to end, one way or the other.

He thought about his parents. Vikram would take good care of them, he had no doubts on that front, but would they ever know how he had died? Would they be able to find his body? Somehow, these thoughts seemed distant, and he couldn't bring himself to care, at least not as much as he cared at the moment for a glass of water.

Suddenly, he heard a distinct click. There was the sound of some sort of a scuffle, a whack and something fell with a thump on the floor above.

A door opened. A floorboard creaked.

All his senses were on full alert as he lay still, scarcely breathing, pretending to be unconscious, praying that whoever it was would go away. He sensed a draught of air and someone drew in a sharp breath. Then there was silence all around. A hand touched his arm and shook him a little. Was it already time for another round? He prayed to God to take his life and end his misery. The small hand shook him again. A small hand?

His eyes snapped open in confusion and he found a young urchin peering down at him, his face close to Nikhil's. He was wearing a monkey cap with only his eyes visible. But those eyes—all he could see was kindness and concern in them. It seemed God had heard his prayers. He had died. Nikhil closed his eyes.

But reality seeped in when the small guy, probably in his teens, began to free him off the ropes on his hands.

"Who are you? What are you doing?" he rasped in Hindi.

"Sh…sh…," the boy whispered, his voice muffled by the monkey cap he wore. One by one all his limbs were free of the ropes. "Just be quiet and follow me." The muffled voice said in Hindi, as the small hands freed him of the electrodes as well.

Nikhil winced and frowned, sure it was another of their tricks, a test. He lay his head back and closed his eyes. "I'm not going anywhere. They'll find both of us and kill you too. Go away." He couldn't have the death of this young boy on his conscience.

"They'll definitely kill us if you don't come with me now. *Right now*." The boy shook Nikhil's shoulder. "Come on, you have to try. I can't do it without your help. Please. Nikhil… Nikhil… come on…" The boy tried to pull him into a sitting position.

"How do you know my name? Why are you helping me?"

"Sh… sh… Can we have this talk later?" he whispered, exasperation evident in his tone.

Nikhil studied his eyes above the monkey cap he wore and sat up with some difficulty. The boy took out a bottle from under the numerous folds of his *phiran* and put it to Nikhil's mouth. He drank the water thirstily, almost choking on it.

"Easy, easy…" The teenager patted his back, as water dribbled down his chin onto his chest. Nikhil began to shiver as the cold registered on his bare body. His savior took off his *phiran*, under which he was wearing another. He also had a plastic bag slung across his chest with a belt, from which he pulled out some clothes.

"Wear these."

"I can wear my own." Nikhil pointed to his shirt and trousers heaped in a corner.

"No." He helped Nikhil pull on the set of *kurta pyjama* he had taken out of the bag, the *phiran*, and then a monkey cap. But he picked up Nikhil's clothes too.

"What… Who—"

"This is not a time to ask questions." He then took off his boots under which he was wearing a pair of worn-out sneakers. He helped Nikhil put on the boots. The plastered leg protested but Nikhil ignored the pain. Hope had begun to surge inside him.

"Can you walk?"

"Yes," Nikhil whispered, his survival instinct taking over. He got to his feet but staggered immediately. His legs refused to support him. Clutching the cot he sat on the plank and took deep breaths willing himself to draw strength somewhere from within. This was his only chance of escape, he couldn't goof it up like this.

"Lean on me, and try to stay behind me." The young boy supported Nikhil with one hand and with the other pointed a gun toward the exit.

From where had he got the gun? Nikhil had no idea. He could swear he had not seen him taking one out of the bag. They moved out of the room then up the stairs, trying not to make any sound, their progress slow and labored.

As they came up the stairs, Nikhil froze, spotting someone lying across the threshold to his freedom.

"Don't worry, he's out cold." The boy stepped over the man.

As Nikhil stepped over the prone figure, he noticed a patch of brown-red blood pooled near the man's head. Had this little guy killed the man?

Nikhil had no time to think, as the boy pulled him forward and he found himself in the corridor encircling the courtyard. Everything was dark and quiet. Luckily, the young boy seemed to know his way around. Staying in the shadows of the corridor, he steered Nikhil toward one of the smaller doors. Then they were out of the house and in the backyard surrounded by high trees.

Silence reigned in the atmosphere. Not a single soul stirred; still the fear of being found out rattled his heart like a stone in an empty tin box. In the mad dash across the open ground to the woods, Nikhil was sure his half-mended leg had broken again, but they managed to reach the relative safety of the cluster of high pine trees.

The boy staggered under his weight as Nikhil's foot stumbled on the loose gravel of the path. "Careful," he muttered, almost falling, but managing to keep them both upright.

Nikhil hadn't anticipated the steep incline of the path going downhill. Life and his situation humbled him as he leaned on the boy like an old man. They walked past the dense trees, whose leaves glistened with dew.

The dark canopy of trees, moist leaves, and the moonless sky gave a sinister edge to the night sounds. But nothing deterred his young savior. He helped Nikhil along the path, determinedly.

"Where are we going?" Nikhil asked when he paused for breath.

The boy didn't answer but marched on propelling Nikhil forward. Nikhil felt his energy ebbing with every step he took, trying to keep his weight off his injured leg. The rough fabric of the *kurta* rubbed over his fresh wounds and made him wince, but he clenched his teeth and ignored the pain.

The boy stopped. Nikhil could make out the outline of a lake just beyond the tree cover. The boy helped Nikhil prop himself up against the tree and handed him the water bottle. "Have some more water and wait here. I'll be back in a few minutes."

A fine mist hung over the lake like a white woolen blanket. After a few minutes the silence, broken only by the crickets, began to play on Nikhil's nerves. The night was turning cold and after the initial surge powered by adrenaline Nikhil's energy was waning fast. Had his escape been discovered? Were they coming after him? Nikhil didn't even know the name of the town or the topography of the place. He had no means of defending himself. Where was the boy? Had he decided to abandon him? Given the state he was in, barely able to walk, Nikhil couldn't blame him if he had.

Just then, he saw the familiar figure emerge from the fog and sighed in relief.

"Follow me," the boy muttered, putting Nikhil's arm over his shoulders once more.

"Where now?" Nikhil straightened from the tree he was leaning on, careful not to put his weight on the plastered leg.

"Just till that bush. We are going to cross the lake."

"You crossed it to come to me?"

The boy nodded, his eyes big and worried under the monkey cap.

Who was this kid?

"The route to the army camp is shortest from here and it is totally wild. They'll not think of following this route. Come on. We don't have time."

Nikhil looked at his throbbing leg, dreading the wave of pain he knew would wash over him the minute he moved it.

"Come on. Don't waste time. It's our lives or your leg. Choose."

The young one was right. Nikhil chose to live. He sucked in his breath and left the support of the tree.

***

The boy had anchored and hidden the small *shikara* used by flower-sellers under a bush on the periphery of the lake. It had a seat for only the rower. He made Nikhil lie down on the floor of the boat with a packet of food.

From his position, Nikhil watched the urchin handle the oars as if he had been born rowing a boat. Everything still appeared surreal. Why was this person helping him? Nikhil had no friends in this place. He didn't even know anyone other than his captors. He peered at the boy but the no-moon night did nothing to aid visibility. In any case, his face was hidden by that hideous cap.

"Who are you?" Nikhil asked again, five minutes into the boat journey.

"You should eat something to get your energy back," he was curtly ordered instead.

The flatbread laden with mint chutney tasted divine. But to his amazement and worry, he didn't have the energy to finish even one. Still, the food, water, and fresh air helped, and he felt energy seeping back into his limbs.

They were halfway across the lake and his little friend was getting tired. Nikhil could make out the labored breathing, though he continued to row with smooth strokes.

"Shall I take one of the oars?"

"They are fixed to the boat. Only one person can row," the boy replied looking alternatively ahead and behind, worried and cautious. "Don't worry, I can do this."

At last, they reached the shore. The teenager jumped down into the water and pulled the *shikara* with a rope. Nikhil crawled out dragging his leg and sat awkwardly on his butt half in the water as the boat wobbled.

The boy giggled softly and helped him to the mossy edge of the lake.

Nikhil lay panting and shivering on the green soft grass. The small activity of disembarking from the boat and crawling a few steps had taken away the little energy he had accumulated on the boat.

"Come on," the little guy was up again, pulling the *shikara* on the grass toward a dilapidated shed a few feet from where Nikhil lay.

"Whose boat is this?" he asked but didn't get any answer.

"Come on, get up." The boy returned from the shed.

"I can't go anywhere now. Just leave me and go. I don't care." Nikhil closed his eyes.

"Please."

"No, I can't," Nikhil said without opening his eyes.

"Look, I can't let my effort go waste just because you are behaving like a child."

The fierce admonition brought a smile to Nikhil's face despite his exhaustion.

"We are in the open. At least take the shelter of the trees." The boy pulled at Nikhil's shoulder again.

"Who are you? Who has sent you?" Nikhil glanced at him.

"You'll get to know that soon. Come on, move. We don't have time. I have to get back home before I'm missed."

"My leg is gone. I can't feel it, let alone move it."

"Lean on me. You can rest for the night once we reach the safe place I have marked in the woods. Come on. Please."

Nikhil sighed and struggled up on his good leg. The boy supported him from the other side and they hobbled into the forest.

"Wait! There's someone near the boat shed," Nikhil exclaimed suddenly.

"Where?" the boy straightened and looked back. "I don't see anyone. Let's go! Time is running out."

He seemed to think Nikhil was trying to delay again, but Nikhil was sure he had seen an old man near the shed. He peered into the darkness. There was no one there. Had he imagined it? It was possible. His nerves were certainly on edge. He allowed the boy to lead him on.

"Are there any animals here?" he asked gritting his teeth and trying not to lean too much on the boy, who, he knew, was tired too.

"Yes, I have heard of some, but have never seen them."

"Maybe this is my lucky night and we won't meet them tonight too." Nikhil mentally crossed his fingers.

"This is it," the boy said, finally coming to a halt.

Unable to support himself and fighting the darkness which seemed to envelop him, Nikhil fell on the forest grounds. As he slithered down the boy's length, his arm brushed against something soft at the boy's chest.

Sprawled on the ground he stared up at the person who had braved all odds and brought him to safety. A pair of midnight-blue eyes with unbelievingly long lashes looked down at him worriedly.

"Are you alright?" the boy asked, not whispering anymore though the voice was still muffled because of the cap.

It was then Nikhil noticed the voice didn't belong to a teenager whose voice had not yet broken, but to a petite girl.

"You are not a boy!"

"Who told you I'm a boy?" The person was amused, Nikhil could tell from the eyes.

"You are a girl!" he shouted.

"Sh…sh…" He, no, she shushed Nikhil like he were a naughty student in her class. And suddenly, he realized that the brusque shushing was quite familiar.

"Sunshine? Doc!" The given names rolled off his tongue, as the shock of the discovery competed with the waves of weakness washing over him. He studied the face of the person who had nursed him for days. The person who had helped him yet again.

She had beautiful eyes.

"How come? How? Why? From where did you get the gun?"

"You can hide here for the night," she continued, disregarding his surprise and questions as usual. She was pointing toward a moss-covered opening in the hill. "I have some food, water, and your medicines, the lotion for the burns and the painkillers. You can take two of them, it'll help you." She held the bag toward him again.

"There is a thin blanket in it. I'm sorry I couldn't bring a heavy one."

He closed his eyes. The wet pyjama clung to his fresh wounds making them sting. "It's fine. You've thought of everything."

"Listen, I don't have time. Stay put, they'll never come and look for you here."

"You sound very sure."

"Yes, I have planted a piece from your shirt on the other way."

Nikhil was speechless at the presence of mind she had displayed and could just stare at her, stunned, as she continued, "Three kilometers downhill from here is my friend Shabnam's house, where I am staying. I'll take you there tomorrow—"

He closed his eyes as the thought finally sank in that he had escaped the torture chamber. He felt himself drifting off into tired slumber.

"Nikhil? Nikhil?!" He jerked awake again as she shook him mercilessly by his shoulders. "Are you listening? Don't you dare die now."

"Yes, yes... don't shake me so much, Sunshine, or I'll break," he rasped as his bones protested at the vigorous movement she was subjecting him to.

"Did you hear what I said?"

"Of course, you'll come tomorrow and take me to Shabnam's house."

"No. Not the house. You will hide in the barn outside the house, actually it's a small shed for sheep."

"Got that."

"Great! I'll meet you tomorrow around one in the night. Is that okay?" She picked up the gun.

"Do you have another?"

"Gun?"

"Yes, from where did you get it?"

"It's not difficult to get a gun in these areas. But I have only one. You can keep it." She offered him the gun.

"No, no…"

"I won't need it. And I have a knife too."

"Give me the knife then."

"No, I'll keep the knife and you keep the gun." She thrust the gun at him again.

"Right now, your wellbeing is more important, else who will rescue me if something happens to you? And I'm equally good with a knife."

Ayesha looked at him. He was lying but was right. She had to make the journey back and come for him again. She took out a knife from her sock and handed it over.

"This a kitchen knife!"

"Yes, but very sharp. And keep this as well." She took off a black thread from her pocket with a silver charm in the middle and tied it around his neck.

"You think I'm going to be safe by wearing this?"

"Yes. Now listen to me carefully. If anyone, other than I… I repeat if anyone finds you here and you are captured, you'll bite on this and chew." She tapped the small silver bullet tied to the black thread around his neck. He could reach it just by touching his chin to the neck.

"What is it?" He frowned at the offending thing. Understanding dawned on his face even as he asked the question, so she didn't answer.

"And if I don't?"

"You'll wish you had never been born," she said, not mincing words.

He looked skywards and closed his eyes.

"It'll be better this way, trust me," she said softly.

He lay back against the soft mossy side of his temporary haven and sighed. "I trust you with my life, Sunshine."

Silently, she arranged the broken branches and leaves at the mouth of the tiny cave so as to keep him warm and hidden, then left.

Nikhil watched her go, not sure if he would see her again. But then that was what he had thought when they had tortured him in the basement. But he had met her again.

Who was she? Why was she putting her life in danger by going against her family? Who was she, this girl with beautiful blue eyes?

***

Scared to the bones, Ayesha negotiated the hilly terrain back to Shabnam's home. She wasn't worried about the people at home because she had spiked their dinner with Nikhil's sleeping pills, but she was wary about this part of the journey. She knew the terrain by heart but nevertheless was scared of running into someone—man or animal. Everything was at stake. She tightened her hold over the gun.

She had planned to complete the return journey to Shabnam's house tonight and had not anticipated that he would be in such a bad shape. It was shocking to see what they had reduced him to in the space of just a few hours. She had seen the fresh burns on his skin when she had removed the electrodes, and the pain etched on every crevice of his face. All her care and efforts gone down the drain.

How she longed to see him healthy and standing on his two feet like he did in the photographs. Somehow, she felt responsible for him. She didn't know why, but she did.

She had planned to help him escape on the last day before they were due to leave for Shabnam's wedding, but Shehzaad had surprised her by moving everything a day earlier.

The way *khala* and she were asked to pack and leave the house, she had guessed that they planned to torture him in the basement. She had been in a bind until she had heard Rehaan telling *khala* about some crisis at the border and Shehzaad had had to leave urgently at midnight. The unexpected play of events gave her the perfect opportunity to plan the rescue. With Shehzaad out of the way and Rehaan sleeping soundly with the other family members, she knew she had a good chance of pulling it off.

It was exhilarating that she had bested Shehzaad and Rehaan.

If she was able to bring Nikhil down to the barn tomorrow, there would be another five-kilometer trek to the nearest road which led directly to the army cantonment. Seeing his condition tonight she had doubts that he would be able to do the complete trek in one night. He would need at least a night's rest in the barn too. She'd have to plan to sneak in food to him.

Thinking of and planning for all the scenarios, and calculating the risks involved, she neared Shabnam's home and the river. Taking a deep sigh she pulled off her *phiran* and kept it in the polybag and set out to cross the river. Her fourth crossing of a water body in a day.

***

CHAPTER EIGHT

Nikhil woke up to the chirping of birds signaling the break of dawn. The nightmare he had woken from slowly transformed into reality as he opened his eyes and heard the forest breathing quietly around him. The birds chirped as did the crickets. The breeze at times made eerie sounds but eased out as the sun began its journey across the horizon. He took a deep breath, clenched his fist around the knife handle and after a while drifted off to sleep again.

It was midday when he woke up again. He felt rested and more alert this time.

'So far so good.' He had survived the night of his escape. The dense canopy of trees sieved the sunlight so it was still dark in the forest.

He cast a glance at his body, clad in beige worn-out traditional attire. Everything except his underwear was borrowed. The blanket lay bunched beneath him. He had drawn it around him and huddled into the earth to ward away the cold seeping into his bones at night. He rubbed his eyes to get rid of the remains of the sleep and winced as he touched his cheek. The wound had not healed completely. He checked his face for any other damage, but everything else seemed fine. His stubble had become a full-fledged beard.

He stirred gingerly in the confined space, but couldn't feel his legs—one was in the cast and the other one was beset with pins and needles. Every movement was an effort. He counted till ten then began to stretch his limbs slowly. The new burns from the previous night and the partially-healed ones from the bomb blast made every movement another kind of torture. Before doing anything else he applied the lotion the girl had left him.

Looking at the bright side, it was a relief that even after the previous night's excursion, apart from his leg in the cast, he could move all his other limbs without any major discomfort. The dislocated shoulder gave him a bit of trouble but it was nothing more than a little muscle abuse.

After ten minutes of getting the blood circulation going in his body, his stomach gurgled. He reached into the bag and took out the leftover *rotis* rolled in newspaper. Last night he had forced himself to eat and had managed to finish only two. There were plenty left. The spicy mint spread over them had kept them soft and palatable. He ate some more, keeping the rest for later, then swallowed a couple of painkillers and decided to explore his surroundings.

The pain had eased off a little, but he still felt weak, so he sat in the tiny cave and fashioned a makeshift cane from a broken tree branch with the knife. The cane would help him move without Sunshine's help. What was her real name? He had forgotten to ask the previous night.

***

Shehzaad was hopping mad. And worried. A feeling which he didn't show to the team but added to his anger.

Rehaan had once again disappointed him. He had gone out, instead of staying in the house as instructed, resulting in a crisis which would become a black mark against Shehzaad's own spotless record. Not only had one of his main men lost his life, but the prisoner had also escaped. There was no forced entry into the house and ropes binding him were not cut, that meant one of the knots came loose and he had escaped on his own.

A prisoner on whom they had spent such a huge amount of money and time. A prisoner whose kidnapping might have been a tactical error in the first place, though he was loath to admit it. After all, he had painstakingly built a reputation of being careful and effective, precisely by not making such kinds of mistakes.

Even so, letting the prisoner escape alive wasn't acceptable. He could be a threat to the entire group's operations. He had to be found first; there would be enough time after that to deal with that good-for-nothing Rehaan.

The fool had inherited nothing from his father, who had been an idol for Shehzaad and many others. He had been given enough leeway thanks to the respect his father had commanded, but it was clear he could not be trusted in deep covert operations. Lazy fool. Altaf's protective hand was on him else Shehzaad would have never taken him under his wing.

"*Bhai*, this was found near the hills, on one of the branches sticking out of the stones of the cliff." One of his men held a torn sleeve of the prisoner's shirt. "I think he has fallen down the hill."

Shehzaad looked at the torn, dirty piece of cloth. "Did you find the body?"

"The cliff is too steep. We can't see to the bottom." The man hesitated, then said, "*Bhai*, there is no way he could have survived the fall."

"Still, keep looking."

Shehzaad smiled when the man had left. It was a lucky break. Further interrogation would have only made it evident to all that he had made an error of judgment in kidnapping Mahajan. But now the man had gone and killed himself in the fog and saved Shehzaad the trouble.

***

The distant clock tower struck the midnight hour. Ayesha got up pretending to go the makeshift toilet near the barn specially constructed for the women of the family. The pillows and her luggage were arranged on the bed as if someone lay there with the blanket pulled over the head.

No one stirred. Shabnam, she knew, slept like a dead sheep, but *khala* worried her. *Khala* was a light sleeper, waking up every now and then due to her weak bladder. The previous night, the sleeping pills had done their work, but Ayesha had given all the remaining medicines to Nikhil and she didn't have any more with her. She waited for another fifteen minutes, then slipped out of the house. The bundle of food was in the barn where she had hidden it in the afternoon.

The water was pretty shallow since the river divided into two streams up in the mountains. This stream was wide, but the flow was mild and tame. She stuffed her long braid inside the salwar suit and pulled on the monkey cap.

Her heart hammered all the way to the forest, both in fear for his safety and in anticipation of meeting him. Last night she had been acutely conscious of his eyes on her and avoided looking at him. Tonight she would look into his eyes and interact with him like an adult. She prayed to the Gods for his life. Despite being on the precipice of death the previous day, he had thought of her safety. Her efforts could not go waste, not when his escape was so near.

As she neared the place she had left him her heart accelerated in anticipation and anxiety. The first wave of panic set in when she couldn't find the cave. Frantically she looked around for the pine tree she had marked with the knife. It took her two minutes and a lifetime of wild heartbeats to locate the tree. She wept with joy when she found the tree and then the cave.

Then she parted the twigs and the second wave of panic hit her. He was gone! Had they got him, so soon? Shehzaad was not back from the border. Rehaan didn't have the brain to search this side of the lake. How could anyone have guessed this route? No, Allah couldn't be so cruel. All her effort, gone down the drain! No, it couldn't happen. She wanted him to live. He had to live. Where had he gone?

She looked around in all directions, looking for some sign of what had happened to him. She couldn't shout or call out his name. The muted, eerie music of the forest was getting to her when she spotted him behind another tree, looking all around in the woods except in her direction.

"What are you doing there?" She marched toward him and hit him on his chest. "Why were you hiding?"

"Hey!"

"How could you hide from me! Do you know I almost d—" Sanity prevailed as he caught hold of her arms.

"Calm down, Sunshine. I just wanted to check if anyone was following you. It's all clear. What happened, sweetheart? Why are you crying?" He ran his thumb over a tear on her cheek visible above the cap.

"Crying?" Shaking off his hands, she stepped back. "I'm not crying. The cold wind makes one's eyes water."

"Really? Are you sure?" He narrowed his eyes.

"Yes. Have you collected everything?" Not meeting his eyes, she picked up a broken branch with leaves and swept the area around the cave to erase their footprints, forgetting all her resolves.

"Why are you wearing this stupid cap again?" Nikhil frowned.

"I'm feeling cold." She adjusted the cap around her neck, scanning the woods.

"I want to see your face."

"Why?" She glanced at him then looked away.

"Why? Isn't it logical?"

"No. Let's go."

"Do you think I'll tell tales about you?" He couldn't help the self-pity which had crept into his tone at her lack of trust and picked up his cane.

"*Allah…* what's the big deal?" She scowled.

"I want to see the one who has saved me. Twice. Is that too much to ask?"

"I'll take it off once we are in the barn. Shall we go now?"

"Yes. What's your name?"

"Ayesha."

He fell silent after that, leaning heavily on the stick, and trying to match her pace. Soon he lagged behind but didn't call out for her to slow down. She stopped once she realized she was going fast for him.

"I'm sorry," she muttered, as he reached her.

"It's okay. How do you know the terrain so well?"

"Shabnam and I bring the sheep to this side in the summers." She slowed down to walk beside him.

He fell silent again. Talking while walking put a strain on his strength. She led him across the forest and they were now walking parallel to the river under the cover of high Chinar trees. The terrain had also eased off a bit. His cane was a big help, though the heavy plaster still made his hip joint ache with each step. After more than an hour Ayesha stopped and moved toward the bank of the river, scanning either direction for signs of life.

"Few yards more," she said.

The ground had panned out into a meadow, making the last few steps less strenuous. Still, Nikhil willed the trek to end. She stopped once again and watched the shed across the river. Beyond the shed, Nikhil could see a simple two-story house near the shore and a few more at a distance.

"Do we have to cross the river?"

"Yes. It's very shallow."

Nikhil groaned inaudibly at the thought of getting his wounds wet again, but nodded and followed her.

The eerie silence all around was periodically broken by chirping crickets. No light or movement could be seen in the house and the surrounding areas. Had he been here under normal circumstances he would have enjoyed the panoramic view of the meadow, but right now his only focus was to keep himself alive… and her out of danger.

"Take off your *phiran* and cap, else it'll get wet." She took hers off too and bundled them into a plastic bag she had brought.

He glanced at her standing still and alert, watching the dwellings on the other side of the river. It seemed she was casting a sleeping spell on all living beings.

Suddenly she said, "We'll cross. The river is pretty tame. Remember to go down on your knees the moment we are out of the water. We'll crawl to the shed. Once there we'll sneak inside from an opening in the back wall. There are sheep inside, so don't get startled."

He sucked in his breath as the cold water hit his legs and then slowly rose to his chest. He watched her wade carefully in the water with the bundle held up on her head. Being shorter, she was in up to her chin and had to struggle to hold her nose up, but nothing deterred her. She was right, though. The flow of water didn't overwhelm them, and they were able to cross easily, albeit at a slow pace.

They crouched as the water began to recede. Nikhil slid on his back and hauled himself out of the water a second time. The shed hid them from the house and they were able to take refuge quickly, startling the sheep. She called out to them softly and they calmed down. Nikhil sank on the floor in one corner of the small room.

"I'm sorry I don't have a spare set of clothes. But the *phiran* is dry and I have hidden a sheet in that hole in the wall, and we also have a *kangri* here." She pulled out the tiny earthen oven, used by the locals to keep warm during the winters.

"This is perfect. They'll dry soon."

"There is a loft which is used to store the hay. You can sleep there peacefully during the day, but I couldn't arrange a ladder. Or you could lie down here, people rarely come into the shed. I'll keep a watch."

"It's fine." He could pull himself up using the nooks and crevices in the crude brick wall during the day.

"There is food, water, lotion, and the painkillers. Whatever happens, just stay out of sight."

"Got that."

"It's another five kilometers trek through the forest to the army camp. I'll come here at the same time tomorrow and take you there," she said rubbing her cheeks dry with her *dupatta*.

He looked at her properly for the very first time in their nine or ten days of association. She didn't match the picture he had created in his mind. She was much younger than he had thought.

Soaked through and through, she had an ethereal charm about her. Her nose-pin twinkled under the faint night light. Though most of her hair was hidden inside her clothes, a few tendrils had sneaked out to frame her face. And she had the most kissable mouth—small and full.

"How old are you?"

"I'll go now. It's late." She ignored him again wrapping a *dupatta* around her head and wore the *phiran*. "We'll start around midnight. Be ready."

Overwhelmed by her sheer courage and tired with the long trek, he nodded and closed his eyes.

***

CHAPTER NINE

"Allahu… Akbarr…" The morning azaan echoing in the valley registered somewhere in Nikhil's mind but he turned over and went to sleep again.

The baa-ing of sheep woke him up after an hour. Someone opened the barn door, and Nikhil shrank into the corner, but the person never entered and all the sheep left the shack. The last one looked at him as if beckoning him to join them, but left when he just smiled.

He had slept like a log for a few hours after Ayesha had left the previous night, but as the effect of medicines began to wear off he had tossed and turned on the hay, biting down the groans escaping his lips, startling the sheep nearest him many a time. The poor animals didn't complain but glanced at him from time to time, as if they empathized with his plight and agony.

Even with these living beings for the company, every movement or sound in the darkness brought on heart-splitting terror. Had his captors caught up with him? Would he be able to swallow the pill before they could stop him? His hand clutched the capsule on his neck as a lucky charm. Dying was better than getting captured again.

Never in his lifetime had he thought there would be a situation where he would consider committing suicide. Life had a strange way of testing one's resolve and strength.

Before the break of dawn, he tried to stand on his feet, but couldn't support his weight. With acute difficulty, he had hobbled to answer nature's call taking the support of the wall. Though he felt relatively clean after the icy dip in the river last night, he still wished for proper facilities.

To keep fear at bay and pass time, he lay down and imagined his reunion with his parents and Vikram. His mother would cry for sure. What about Vikram? Would Vikram cry? His accident in Ladakh had brought them together but the implicit trust Vikram had placed in him over the years had bonded them forever. Mrs. Seth, Vikram's mom, called them soul brothers. And would he, himself, cry? Maybe, maybe not. He wasn't sure about anything at the moment. The ordeal had humbled him. In his arrogance, he had never thought about the limitations of his strength and his control over situations.

As the day wore on, Nikhil got extremely uncomfortable and hot. It seemed he was coming down with fever. He had finished the chapatis and pickle, which Ayesha had left last night, but he longed for a hot cup of ginger tea.

His breath hitched when the barn door opened without any warning. All his discomforts and pain receded, and he burrowed deep into the bed of hay, hoping he was invisible to the intruder.

"Hey, it's me," she whispered.

The relief made him close his eyes and thank all kind of Gods.

"You must be hungry. I'm sorry, I could bring only this." She opened the newspaper packet and lay it beside him. "And here are some more painkillers, these will last for another two days, by that time you'll be well on your way."

He sat up brushing the hay and wincing at the pain in his joints and the half-mended fracture. Spread before him was a loaf of bread and vinegar-soaked onions. "It's great, but you shouldn't have bothered. I don't feel like eating." He supported his head on the wall behind and closed his eyes.

"You don't feel like eating? How come? Are you not feeling well?" She touched the back of her hand to his arm and immediately took it away. "You are burning! Again!"

He grimaced.

"How will we go tonight? You are not fit enough to stand, let alone walk five kilometers."

"I can, and I will. I'll be fine by midnight."

"Let me see if I can find some antibiotic. You better get something in your stomach before taking the medicine." She nudged the newspaper toward him and ran out.

Nikhil forced himself to eat a few bites of the loaf and finish the entire bottle of water. The smell of onions made him gag so he pushed them away and lay down again. Sleep helped him forget his misery.

When Ayesha came two hours later, he was sleeping, his breathing erratic. She didn't have the heart to wake him and stood looking down at him. Would she be able to take him to safety before Rehaan or *khala* caught on?

Rehaan had come in the morning in a frenzy. Ayesha had kept her fingers crossed as he and his men had searched the entire village, all except his own uncle's house. She had banked on this fact. Since Shabnam was getting engaged and the house was brimming with relatives, he hadn't felt the need to search the house, and he had forgotten about the shed for the time being.

Nikhil sighed bringing her back to the present. If he wasn't well tonight, they wouldn't be able to go. The entire path was downhill, and he would find the trek difficult with his leg in the cast.

She placed the antibiotic tablets near his head and hoped he would take them when he woke. She wasn't sure if she would be able to come again. It was becoming increasingly difficult for her to make excuses to *khala* to run to the shed or to the market.

***

Nikhil found the tablets and the full bottle of water next to his head when he woke again. He took one and slept again.

She came again in the afternoon as the sheep were being shepherded into the barn and sat down at the door.

"Shabnam, the other day when you had taken the antibiotic, the dose was one tablet three times a day, right?" She addressed someone outside loudly in Hindi. It served as a warning for him, as well as informed him about the dosage of the medicine.

"Yes, why?" a girl asked.

"I was just having an argument with Asma on the dosage. And why didn't you wake me up in the morning? I told you I wanted to go with you."

"Who was sleeping like she was dead?" the girl grumbled. "I tried to wake you for a full ten minutes, but you didn't even stir. Wanted to pour a bucketful of water on your head, but you were sleeping in my bed."

Ayesha chuckled. "You should have poured it on me. I had to spend the whole morning with *khala* rolling out *seviyaan* for your engagement. Even after washing twice my hands still smell of flour and *ghee*."

"Good for you. The way you were sleeping, it seemed as if you had spent the entire night with your lover."

There was a meaningful pause. He could imagine Ayesha glaring at Shabnam, aware that he must have heard. How he wished he could see her in that moment.

"Really," Ayesha recovered fast, "…and who gave you classes on all these things? Zeenat *khala?*"

Both the girls giggled and joked about their unmarried *khala*, teasing each other good-naturedly, comfortable in each other's company.

She didn't come during the night. But someone else did.

***

Late in the evening, Nikhil had crawled out through the back door to the river to answer nature's call.

It was then that he heard them.

His heart rate quickened. There were two of them snooping inside the shed. Taking a firm hold on the gun Ayesha had left him, he tried to recall if there was anything in the shed that could give him away. Apart from the dusty blanket and water bottle, the only thing that could raise their suspicions was the medicine which he had hidden in one of the grooves in the wall. He hoped they wouldn't be able to spot them in the darkness.

After a few minutes, talking between themselves they came out and walked around the shed toward him. Adrenaline kicked in as he curved his forefinger around the trigger.

If he gunned them down he would bring the entire household upon him. Or… Taking a lungful of air he went into the river. Shivering he lay in the shallow waters as the men stood a few feet from him. Underwater, his pulse drumming in his ears didn't allow him to hear anything they said.

Still talking, thankfully they moved a few steps away with their backs to him. His lungs were about to burst, as he lifted his head above the water and took a deep breath, then went down again.

"Rehaan!"

Nikhil heard Ayesha. They turned toward her as she came running from the house and Nikhil was able to take another breath. The tall man muttered something to his partner who walked off toward the main gate.

"Hey, *jaan!*" The man, whom Ayesha called Rehaan, said.

The breeze carried his voice toward Nikhil who had come out of the river. The endearment froze him in the process of crawling out of the water.

"Rehaan, where were you? I was looking for you the whole day!" she said.

Rehaan stood looking at her, then said, "You know this is the first time I find you so eager to see me. Is it because of my absence? If that's the case, I won't hover around you so much, Ayesha." His voice was heavy with lust.

"Come, let's have dinner."

"Why are you so afraid of me, love?"

"Rehaan, please." She sounded breathless and actually scared.

"Please what? Don't you like me touching you?" he said huskily.

"Someone might see," she objected, then sucked in her breath as if in pain.

Nikhil's fingers curled into a fist as he heard the rustle of clothes and the man moan. He felt like ramming the knife into him.

"Rehaan, please," Ayesha pleaded. "*Khala* will be very angry if we are late."

The man sighed. "Okay fine. Looking at the celebrations today, I feel like asking *ammi* to plan our *nikah* soon."

The conversation faded as they moved toward the main house.

Nikhil crawled back to the shed, trying to ignore the information, but the conversation refused to leave him. *Nikah*? Rehaan and Ayesha were a couple, about to get married? She was getting married to the brute who had manhandled her? How had she consented to the marriage? Did she even like him?

He shook his head. What was it to him? Why was he even thinking about the people here? This was just a mirage. How had a level-headed person like him become so fanciful? It was time he got back to his own life. And allowed her to get back to hers. He took the medicine and tried to sleep.

*****

CHAPTER TEN

She came in the afternoon with food and water hidden under her *phiran*. "Are you okay? Can you walk tonight?"

"Want to get rid of me?" He looked at her as he sat taking the support of the wall behind him.

"Yes," she said, dropping her gaze on the food packet in her hand.

"Why?"

"You ask too many questions."

"Isn't it natural under the circumstances?"

"The less you know about me the better." She glanced at him as if waiting for him to counter her statement.

"How old are you?" he asked instead.

"Guess," she challenged playfully. She sat at the threshold of the barn with her *dupatta* wrapped around her head in the local tradition, playing with one of the lambs, as if she had all the time in the world.

"Twenty."

She chuckled and shook her head.

"Nineteen."

She began to laugh soundlessly, shaking with her hand on her mouth.

"Come on." He smiled despite the fatigue and the situation. "Don't tell me you are younger."

"No. No." She hiccupped in between the laughter. "I'm twenty-two."

"No way!"

"Yes. I just look like that… small."

"You look beautiful," he said softly.

The easy atmosphere changed into an uncomfortable silence as they stared at each other. A sheep shuffled, breaking the moment.

He sighed. "We'll go tonight." He wasn't feeling that well, yet he wanted it to be over and didn't want her to take any more risks on his account. The number of relatives in the house was increasing day by day. She had told him she had given them sleeping pills the first night when there were a handful of them, but now it was not an option.

He couldn't control himself and asked another question. "From where did you get this?" He held out the charm on his neck.

"My father gave it to me."

"Why would a father give poison to his own child?" He scowled, looking at the offending thing.

"The circumstances were difficult, and we were traveling from PoK to this side of the border and every day we used to hear various stories."

"Where are your parents now? And why have you been carrying this with you?"

She sighed. "They are dead. They died during our journey here."

"Oh! I'm sorry."

"It's okay, it has been many years."

"You should have destroyed it much earlier. Keeping this is dangerous. Or do you still fear someone out here?"

"No, no. I'm alright. *Khala* is quite affectionate. It's just… kind of a memento. It's harmless unless one chews really hard on it."

"And why are you helping me?"

"I don't know."

"Please don't lie."

"Oh really, I'm lying now? And you know everything? Okay… so you tell me the truth. Why am I helping you?"

"You have fallen deeply and irrevocably in love with me, and can't see me dead," he smiled.

"Really?!" she chuckled, not meeting his eye, tucking a non-existent strand of hair behind her ear.

"Yes." He looked at her solemnly and added. "And I'm falling for you right at this moment." He couldn't control himself and opted for the truth.

The grin faded from her lips and she dropped her eyes to her hands clasped in her lap.

"And I don't want to leave you. I don't care if they find me and kill me," he said, despite the numerous lectures he had given himself the previous night.

"You are delirious," she said.

"No, I have never been more aware of my emotions for another human being. Ever."

"You are having that syndrome… I'm forgetting the name…which the victim has toward his kidnapper … "

"Stockholm Syndrome."

"Yes, that's the name!"

"As per Stockholm Syndrome, I should be falling in love with your fiancé."

Her glance jerked to him, but she recovered fast.

She chuckled and said, "No...? Then I guess it's called transference or some such psychological term. Yes. That's it. Don't worry. Once you are back in your world everything will be fine."

"I suspect nothing will ever be right after this is over." He lay his head on the hay and closed his eyes. "Can't you say no to the alliance if you don't like him?"

"Who said I don't like him?"

"I heard everything yesterday, Sunshine," he said without opening his eyes.

She saw disapproval etched on his face as if she was to blame, and bristled. Who was he to question her? She stood up.

"Where are you going?" His gaze jerked to her.

"It's time. I'll come back around midnight. Be ready." She ran out of the barn without giving him a chance to protest or to extend the conversation.

The tears came the moment she entered Shabnam's room. There was no one in the room, and she was soon crying her heart out.

Why had he been captured and brought to her? He had ignited a yearning in her for a better life, one she had never thought possible. A better life with a better man. A better man...? Better than whom? What kind of a man did she want? How could she compare? She didn't know him. She didn't know anything about him. He was just fulfilling a fantasy she had never thought to dream of before. As she heard someone coming up, she sniffled and tried to bring her emotions in control. Just this one night, then everything would be back as it was before.

"There you are!" Huffing and puffing, *khala* entered the room. "I have been looking for you the whole afternoon and you are hiding here. What happened? Are you crying? What's wrong with you, girl? Half the time you are yawning or crying? And why are you washing so many clothes? Answer me, Ayesha," she snapped.

"They got stained," Ayesha gave the excuse she had ready.

"Stained? Oh…" Comprehension dawned and she became slightly sympathetic. "Then wash just the lowers, why the *kurta* as well. Clothes will not dry so easily in this weather."

Ayesha nodded and *khala,* in a rare show of sympathy, left her alone forgetting the reason she had come upstairs.

***

Ayesha sneaked out again a little after midnight. Nikhil was awake and waiting for her. He was looking better but was uncharacteristically quiet. The last few days had changed him.

"Ready?"

"Yes."

They sneaked out of the shed and crossed the river once again. They walked in silence in the shelter of the trees but parallel to the river for easy navigation. He didn't attempt to start a conversation again as if he were angry with her. She fingered her ring in agitation. Who was he to judge her? And who had asked for his opinion? Let him sulk.

"Hold it!"

The voice froze them in their tracks. For a moment Ayesha's heart stopped beating.

"Hands on your head."

She put her hands up and looked at Nikhil, who had dropped his stick and held his hand up. It was then she remembered that she had given the gun to Nikhil.

"Turn around," the man shouted. "Slowly."

The voice sounded familiar. She turned and saw two men, each brandishing a rifle, one pointed at her and the other at Nikhil's chest. She recognized one of the men. He was from her neighborhood, about her age or younger. She had celebrated Eid and other festivals with his mother and sister. What was he doing here? Was he part of Rehaan's group too?

"What are you doing on this side of the river and at this time?"

"Rehaan has sent me." She hoped her voice was muffled enough to pass for that of a man.

"Rehaan? Take off the cap."

Her heart hammering, she slowly pulled off the woolen cap.

"Ayesha?" the man hissed.

"Ali," she whispered, not knowing what else to say.

He looked so shocked it would have been comical under normal circumstances.

"What are you doing here?" he asked, then turned to his companion, "Put the rifle down, I know her."

The man aiming at Ayesha lowered his rifle, though Ali continued to keep his own weapon trained on Nikhil.

Ayesha didn't know what to answer. There must be others around too. She would die now. They would both die—Nikhil and her.

Then everything happened at once. Ayesha felt something whistle past her face and Ali's partner slumped down, clutching his chest. In the next instant, Nikhil had tilted Ali's gun upwards and lunged at him.

"Get down!" Nikhil shouted to her, then slashed the knife across Ali's throat. Blood spurted out and Ali slumped forward, choking and gurgling.

Despite Nikhil's warning, Ayesha stood where she was like a statue staring at the blood running down Ali's chest and soaking his *phiran* to a maroon color. How did the knife appear so fast in Nikhil's hand?

"Get down… ah…" Nikhil pulled her down behind a tree, then groaned again. "You are an idiot," he panted, then cursed, clutching his leg. "When I say get down, you get down!" he whispered fiercely, looking out the woods beyond their hiding place. "Do you have a friend with you today?"

"No." She still couldn't take her eyes away from Ali bleeding on the mossy, uneven earth.

"Then who could have saved us?"

"Saved us?" She looked around in a daze.

"Snap out of it, Ayesha."

She looked at him. It was surprising to see Nikhil so agile and alert. She never thought he could move so fast.

Leaning heavily on the walking stick, he picked up the rifles.

"Get a grip and think. Who could have come to our rescue? Can you think of anyone who would help you?"

"No." She stared again at Ali.

Nikhil let the puzzle be for the moment. If there was anyone watching over them, he or they would expect them to move out of the danger zone quickly.

"Should we hide the bodies? I saw a crevice behind that tree. We can put them there and cover them with leaves," he said.

"Yes," she said, looking all around.

"Come on…"

They dragged the bodies and dropped them in the fissure between the two pine trees and hurriedly covered them with whatever they could find. His leg had begun throbbing again and he leaned heavily on the cane. He turned to see she was muttering a silent prayer, her hands spread together in front of her chest.

The moment she opened her eyes, Nikhil caught hold of her arm and prodded her to move. "Come on, let's go!"

She spared a last glance at the place they had hidden Ali, then followed Nikhil downhill. In a few minutes, she took the lead again.

***

After half an hour of relentless walking, Nikhil paused to rest, taking the support of a tree. "Are you okay?" He looked at her, but she refused to meet his eyes. "Ayesha?"

She glanced at him, then looked away. "I knew him," she whispered, after a moment's pause.

"Yes, I understood that."

"His name is… was… Ali."

"Okay."

"He is dead because of me," she whispered. It was a statement which showed neither relief or fear, just plain resignation.

"No, he is dead because he sided with the wrong people. And had he not died, it would have been us lying in that hollow," he said.

"Yes." She began to shiver and rubbed her arms.

He had a colossal urge to take her into his arms and comfort her. He wasn't sure how she would take it if he hugged her. He watched helplessly as she continued to rock, her body refusing to obey her mind. She looked so lovely with her fair skin and blue eyes, it seemed anything that touched her would spoil the beauty, including him.

"Why are you so distressed today? You killed that man in the house, but now—"

She pivoted toward him, her eyes huge on her face. "I didn't kill him! I just hit him with a rock. He wasn't dead, he was just knocked out!"

Sensing her distress, he agreed immediately, "Of course."

"Did you think he was dead?" she asked wringing her hands.

"No, no… of course not. There was not enough light in the house."

"I just hit him on the head."

He looked into the misted deep eyes and regretted bringing up the subject. "It's okay. I think he was just unconscious."

She tried to breathe deeply and get some control over her senses. The nose pin glinted in the moonlight. "He is very young… was very young," she corrected herself. "Younger than me."

"I'm sorry."

"His mother will never see him."

"It was either him or us, Ayesha. It is the only rule of survival."

"Survival? Yes. Only survival." She closed her eyes.

Nikhil looked at the beautiful girl—troubled and grieving. The death had hit her hard. His gaze, kind and sympathetic, roamed all over her face framed by the rebellious curls that had escaped her *phiran*. He lifted a hand to touch the fair, smooth cheek.

It was then she realized she didn't have her cap on. She stepped back immediately and looked around. The magic around him faded making him aware of his aches and pains.

"I must have dropped it!"

"What?" He frowned.

"The cap."

He took out the cap from the over-sized pocket of his *phiran* and held it out to her. She took it and put it on, hiding her pain and anguish behind the grey wool.

"Let's go."

They began the downhill trek again. After half an hour, she paused near a cluster of trees. The lights from the army cantonment were visible in the distance. The time had come for them to part ways. He handed over the gun and knife to her.

"Remember, don't give your name to anyone except the highest officials. The media shouldn't get a whiff of your name or appearance. You have to remain in hiding, else they'll come after you again," she said looking at the gate from behind the tree.

From the way she rattled off the instructions, some of which hadn't even occurred to him, a seed of doubt began to take root that there was more to her than she let on. But he nodded, looking at her, unwilling to spoil the moment with details. "So, when do we meet again?" he whispered, interrupting her.

"We can never meet again!" The steel in her voice matched the steel in her soul with which she had orchestrated his escape.

"Okay. Can you take off your cap?"

"Why?"

"Just once, I want to look at you… only once."

He lifted his hand to remove the stupid monkey cap, but she stepped back.

"No." She took another step back. "Go and forget about everything. It's for the best. For both of us."

"Sunshine—"

"Do you want to see me dead?"

"No!"

"Then go. Forget the days you have spent here. Go… time is running out. Dawn is about to break. I'll have no time to go back if I loiter here babysitting you."

He could see the smile in her blue eyes.

"Why don't you come with me?"

"Do you want to see me dead?" she asked again.

She was emotionally blackmailing him, but he also knew she was right. Both of them couldn't disappear at the same time. They might not hunt him, but they would definitely hunt and kill her. Ego and fanaticism went hand in hand.

"Go, I'm watching," she muttered.

He sighed, swallowed the ache in his throat and began to walk away. Something glinted in the faint moonlight when he turned to look at her again. She stood there in the same pose, with that monkey cap on, looking like an overgrown street urchin with deep-blue eyes.

It was time to leave but something nagged at his mind; it was like he was leaving unfinished business behind. The feeling persisted as he turned toward his destination. The trek was uneven, but he managed to navigate it with the help of his walking stick.

He walked across the few yards of the forest toward his freedom, leaving behind his guardian angel. He walked across the road to the army cantonment fence leaving behind a piece of his soul. His chest, it seemed, would explode but for the heavy weight pressing on his lungs.

He turned back when he reached the gates, but couldn't locate her. All he could see were the woods. She was somewhere there, probably returning to her cousin's barn. It was for the best. He sent a silent prayer up to God Almighty to keep her safe and happy.

Then, the moment of bittersweet peace was gone. All hell broke suddenly loose when he took off his monkey cap and approached the army guards at the gate.

He couldn't see beyond the floodlight and torchlights aimed at him. Stern voices instructed him to keep his hands above his head. He was sure that all the guns were trained on him too.

He raised his hands and asked for the officer-in-charge.

***

CHAPTER ELEVEN

After a thorough security check, Nikhil was made to wait in the guard room at the gate for half an hour until the Captain arrived.

"What's your name?" he barked in Hindi, annoyed to be woken up in the wee hours of the morning. Nikhil knew he looked a sight with the bandages, the uncombed, matted hair, the unkempt beard, and the borrowed half-torn local clothes.

"We need to talk somewhere private," Nikhil said in English.

The effect of the language was immediate. The officer frowned in surprise and looked at other guards in the room.

"He is clean," one said.

The officer narrowed his eyes, studying Nikhil for a few seconds then said, "Follow me."

Nikhil painfully followed him dragging his broken leg, leaning heavily on the makeshift stick. The officer didn't make any attempt to help him. Nikhil didn't expect any. The officer took him to a basement interrogation room, which had a two-way mirror. Uniformed guards stood outside the room.

"Well?" he asked when Nikhil sat down groaning, on one of the two chairs.

"My name is Nikhil Mahajan, assistant to Vikram Seth, the industrialist. Since the bomb blast in Kamathipura, Mumbai, I have been in the captivity of some terrorist group and have escaped somehow. And at the moment, I don't think my escape should be made known to anyone, especially the media."

His disclosure brought a visible change on the Captain's face.

After that everything happened very fast. The officer made a call to someone from the basement phone, then asked Nikhil about his needs.

The first thing Nikhil asked for was a doctor. His leg was hurting as if it had been severed and he thought he was running a temperature too. The first thing that the doctor ordered was a large glass of lemonade and paracetamol. Nikhil was severely dehydrated, he was told. Sipping the drink from the glass reminded him of Ayesha and the straw meals. She had been quite innovative in coming up with palatable drinks and broths.

The army doctor was examining him when a middle-aged, distinguished-looking man entered the doctor's room.

"Mr Mahajan, K. N. Rao, IB," the man said, shaking his hand.

Surprised at his arrival so soon, Nikhil studied Rao as he took his health report from the doctor. Not even an hour had passed since Nikhil's declaration and the IB had sent their man. Was Rao stationed somewhere near?

"Thanks, doctor. We'll take it from here." Rao shook hands with the doctor. "Will he be able to walk?"

"I can't say too much without the x-ray. I'll arrange for a stretcher. The broken leg has been abused and neglected. He shouldn't put any weight on it," the doctor said.

Rao nodded and took Nikhil to a waiting helicopter, as soon as the stretcher was arranged.

"Where are we going?" Nikhil asked Rao once they were airborne.

"Delhi. Hospital, then the safe house."

"You can drop me at Vikram's farmhouse. It is safer than any other place I can think of. There's even a helipad available."

"No one should know you are back till the time we have completed the debrief process. A safe house is better. Rest assured Vikram and your parents will be informed in due course."

"But…"

"Mahajan please… your escape has already cost my best man three days' worth of effort."

"Cost? Your man?" Nikhil frowned, then comprehension dawned. "So it was your man who saved us from those two in the forest? Did you know about me being kept there? You knew I was there, and yet—"

"Whoa… hold on… " Rao held up his hands. "My man was stationed there for some reconnaissance. He happened to notice the activity near the lake. He recognized you when you slit that man's throat. And after that, he was continuously guarding you… and her."

"Her?"

"The girl who helped you escape. You must have made quite a profound impression for her to go against her own people."

Nikhil pursed his lips and tried to rein in his concern, but lost the battle and asked softly, "Is she back home safe?"

"Yes."

Nikhil didn't meet Rao's eyes as the latter gazed piercingly at him.

***

Rao looked up as Karan sauntered into the waiting area outside the examination room of the agency-run hospital in Delhi. He was one of Rao's best. The best ever.

Karan sighed and sat down keeping the distance of one seat between them.

"You know what you have to do," he said looking at the poster on the wall.

"Why me?" Karan scowled, crossing his arms.

"Because you are the only person who is privy to this, and I intend to keep it that way." Rao slid an envelope on the seat between them.

"I'm not a babysitter," Karan protested despite knowing that his boss seldom changed his orders.

"Mahajan doesn't really need a keeper. It's only till his leg heals. Consider it as a well-deserved holiday."

Karan snorted and picked up the envelope.

***

Nikhil was admitted into the hospital with an identification number on his prescription. No name was mentioned by anyone. He was surprised to see the date on the paper. It had been almost a month since the bomb blast. According to his estimate, it should have been three weeks. He had been unconscious or delirious for four days under Ayesha's care, then had spent another six to seven days in the basement, and then there was the one night when he was tortured. Then he had spent four nights in the forest and the barn. Did they take a full week to transport him from Mumbai to Pulwama after the blast? Or had he lost all sense of time?

The doctor's questions brought Nikhil back to the present. No history was discussed, only the symptoms. The doctor ran the necessary tests, x-rayed his leg and examined his wounds, which were re-bandaged. After a wait of four hours, he put on a fresh cast, less bulky than before, and pronounced Nikhil fit enough to convalesce at home, albeit with a long list of dos and don'ts and another list of medicines. His fresh wounds would take at least two weeks to heal and the leg would take another four weeks before the cast could be removed.

Rao was waiting outside when Nikhil came out of the examination room in a wheelchair. A man sat beside him looking at his phone.

Rao stood up and gestured toward the man who seemed least interested in him. "This is Karan. He'll take care of you until I say otherwise."

"Take care?" Nikhil scowled and looked at the tall lanky man, in his late twenties, dressed in an open leather jacket, his Aviators hooked on the neck of his t-shirt. The man looked more like a spoilt brat rather than an officer. He stood up a bit reluctantly and extended his hand. The handshake was firm yet impersonal.

"You will follow whatever Karan says without question," Rao added, addressing Nikhil.

"What's that supposed to mean?"

"It means you are to behave like my pet," Karan smirked.

"Am I supposed to wag my tail and lick his face too?" Nikhil scowled at Rao.

"Cool it, you two. It's nothing like that. Karan is an expert on the Kashmir issue and has direct access to the latest data from the field operatives. You being in the security profession, I hope I don't have to stress upon the necessity of establishing a chain of command. I want you to rest for two-three days, then we'll talk. In the meantime, please do not try to contact anyone, not your parents, nor Vikram Seth."

Nikhil nodded curtly.

Karan drove a white hatchback to a busy locality of New Delhi, which had a series of multi-story housing apartments with a number of exits, a perfect place to lose a trail if needed. They entered the two-bedroom apartment on the first floor, with a spacious living area and an adequate kitchen.

"You can take this bedroom," Karan gestured toward the bedroom to the left of the living room. "There are two entry and exit points. The second one is the window in the bathroom, which leads to the fire escape and, if the situation gets tough we can also remove this glass pane and jump." He tapped the fixed glass window in the lobby area. "If anyone asks, you are my cousin and your name is Ramprasad."

"What did you say?" Nikhil asked incredulously.

"There are two exits—"

"The name." Nikhil cut in, and Karan grinned.

"Ramprasad."

"Really?"

"Yes, that is what it says on the ID the agency has provided." He tossed the envelope onto the side table.

"That was the best the agency could come up with?"

"We are not known for pandering to the sophisticated sensibilities of a certain class of people," Karan retorted.

"Why do I detect a bit of disdain for me?" Nikhil stared at Karan, who had the grace to look a bit sheepish as he opened the fridge.

"Want some beer?" Karan asked calling for a truce.

Nikhil sighed, too tired to engage in a trivial conflict. "No thanks. A bath is what I need." He was still wearing the clothes the army had provided him at the cantonment in Pulwama.

"We have stocked some clothes in all sizes. You'll find them in the wardrobe in your room. Feel free to use anything you like."

Nikhil took the packet to his room and tore open the yellow envelope. A voter's ID card in the name of Neal Mehra spilled out onto the bed.

"Bastard!" he muttered and smiled.

In the bathroom, he stripped off his clothes and looked in the mirror for the first time since the day of the bomb blast in Mumbai. He couldn't recognize the man staring back at him in the mirror. His hair, matted with dirt, was stuck to his skull. The only things which were clean were his wounds and the skin around it which had been taken care of by the hospital nurse.

He had a full-fledged beard with a patch of bandage where the skin on his face had burned. The scar would definitely leave a reminiscence of…? Of what? What should he call the events of the past weeks? An incident? An episode? A misfortune? He drew a blank. In retrospect, past few weeks seemed like something which could not be explained in words.

Pushing his confused thoughts aside he examined his leg. The burns were deeper on the shin and thigh, the doctor had told him. He looked gaunt, a shadow of his former self. He must have lost at least ten kg, if not more. Sighing audibly, he unwrapped the new toothbrush and remembered his own electrical one in his bathroom back home.

Everything unfamiliar, and every person a stranger. A new name. A new identity. His ordeal was far from over. He picked up the new tube of the toothpaste and felt like a beggar.

Taking the support of the wall, head bent down, he stood under the shower with the water running down his face, and wept. The adrenaline rush of keeping himself alive receded as he emptied the fears, worries, and helplessness of the past month down the drain with the bathwater. The thought of being able to see his parents soon made him more emotional. He sniffed and sniveled, and resolved to take back control of his life. And most of all, he resolved to do something about those monsters back in the Tral forest.

He was perfectly composed and in control when he limped out of the room—squeaking clean, dressed in a fresh t-shirt and shorts.

Karan was sprawled on the sofa reading the newspaper. "Feel better?"

"Yeah, thanks."

"There's food in the kitchen. The maid comes morning and evening. She has a key and we leave instructions for her on the tiny whiteboard in the kitchen. I don't have to remind you to not speak to her or anyone else about anything. You are my cousin and have come here for treatment. And I am a journalist and work in Daily News, Delhi office."

"Hmm…" Nikhil opened the fridge to inspect the contents. "You report directly to Rao?"

"Why?"

"Just curious." He picked up a plate and loaded it with food, his first proper meal in ages if one discounted the cold plate of rice and curry at the army camp and the sandwich at the hospital.

"We have a reporting hierarchy."

Nikhil smiled. He had not really expected Karan to share anything with him.

"You belong to Delhi?" Nikhil asked as he settled on the bar stool at the kitchen counter.

"Nope."

"Do I get a phone or a laptop?"

"Nope."

"So, I am a prisoner here."

"Nope."

"How am I supposed to pass time?" Nikhil gritted his teeth.

"TV is yours. It has all kinds of subscriptions."

Nikhil left it at that and dug into his food, but found himself unable to swallow more than a couple of spoonfuls. Nothing tasted palatable. The medicines and his fever had affected his taste buds. Taking deep breaths he forced himself to eat, longing to get better and strong as soon as possible.

"You can't have a phone, but you can have this." Karan came up and placed a gun with a silencer on the counter.

"Do you know who they are?"

Karan remained silent, which meant he knew.

"Do you think they have this kind of a reach?"

"It's just a precaution."

***

CHAPTER TWELVE

Tired from the back-breaking work during Shabnam's engagement, Ayesha sighed imperceptibly as khala and she took the bus back home. She couldn't wait to lie down on her own bed. There had been so many people in Shabnam's house that on the last two nights she hadn't even got a proper bed to lie down. She had had to squeeze herself between Shabnam and her little sister on their narrow mattress on the floor to get any rest.

Rehaan was not at home. The house was locked. Taking a long breath, she opened the house with their keys. Memories of that night came rushing back to her. She could never forget the smell of fear as she had struck the man unconscious, and the image of Nikhil tied to the plywood plank with electrodes attached to his skin with burnt skin around them. Her gaze went to the basement door the moment she entered, and she froze!

"What happened to the basement?" she blurted. The opening was gone and there was a wall instead—freshly painted.

"What basement?" *khala* said, not meeting her eyes.

"*Khalajaan?*"

"Oh… ho. It was of no use. And it was gathering dust, so Rehaan thought to seal it. Once and for all."

"What happened to the man?" Ayesha asked feigning innocence.

"Now listen to me girl. I know you have seen a lot, but it'll do no good to us and you if you ever mention him or the basement to anyone. Just wipe it out of your memory. There is no basement in this house. There never has been. Understood?"

She nodded.

"And there was no man," *khala* added.

Prodded by *khala* she overcame her surprise and went to clean the bedroom for the night.

Rehaan came back two days later, looking worried and depressed. He seemed to have lost weight too. He had been demoted in the chain of command, but *khala* wasn't worried; he was the blue-eyed boy—son of their slain leader and nephew of the current leader of the group. Riding the high of Shabnam's engagement, she began to plan Rehaan and Ayesha's wedding.

***

Ayesha sat soaking the afternoon sun near the lake. She loved this time of the day, spent in solitude at her personal haunt under the tree. Hidden from prying eyes by the woods, she got a few hours of respite from the daily work and chaos at home.

The green expanse of the meadow glistened after the previous night's rain. The breeze slowly rippled her hair, blowing it away from her face. She had washed her hair and was gently detangling it with her fingers when she heard the muffled footsteps. Arranging her *dupatta* around her head, she turned and forgot to breathe.

Hands in the pockets of his jeans and with black t-shirt stretched tight across his chest, he sauntered toward her without any support. His leg had mended. The scar on his cheek glistened in the sunlight, fully healed. How had he come here? How had he recovered so fast? Was it a dream? She blinked but he kept walking toward her.

Heart in her mouth, she stood up with a jerk when he was two feet away. "What… what are you doing here?" She looked around, anxiously. There was no one in sight.

A faint smile playing on his lips, he stopped right in front of her, unconcerned that anyone would spot him.

"I had told you not to come here. Why have you come back? Did you bring any security with you?"

"Relax. Everyone's busy."

She looked around, indeed there was absolute silence. Even the birds had stopped chirping as if they were enjoying a siesta after a hard day's work.

"Come, we never had a chance together." He took her arm and guided her toward the thick canopy of trees. "Today is for just you and me."

Confused, she followed him. He took her deep inside the forest. Her heart oscillated like a pendulum between ecstasy and bewilderment. She wanted to be with him, yet worried someone might spot them.

"This is enough." She stopped near an ancient tree and stood with her back to it. "Let's just get this over with. Then you should go back immediately."

He studied her, feature by feature. She leaned back as he tucked a stray strand of hair behind her ears. "You have got beautiful hair."

"*Allah*, have you come here to talk about my hair?"

"I saw your face, but your hair was always hidden."

"This is ridiculous." She kept looking around. "I don't even have a gun. Are you armed?"

"Forget everything and look at me," he said, caressing her cheek.

She turned to him. He had moved closer invading her personal space, but she wasn't bothered. Her worry faded as she looked into his eyes, a tantalizing shade of coffee. Involuntarily her hand went to the scar on his cheek. More than an inch of oval puckered, pink skin, a reminder of the episode that had brought them together, yet one which she would like to forget.

He moved his hand to the nape of her neck and brought his lips down on hers—his skin cool against hers. Clutching the tree against her back, she tried not to respond, but her heart galloped as he moved his lips coaxing hers apart. His desperate sigh sent shivers down her body making her forget everything around them. The need of the hour was just to give in to whatever he demanded.

Breathless and longing for closer contact, she threw caution to the winds and left her hold on the tree trunk. She felt him smile as she put her arms around his neck, he then tenderly gathered her close to him. In that moment nothing remained hers. It was a total surrender, but there was no loser.

She wanted the moment to continue forever. It was like there was no one but them in the whole world. Alone, together, with only trees and lakes for a company.

A shot rang out, startling them. She tried to push him away, but he didn't let her go and continued to kiss her cheeks, jaw, neck.

"Nikhil?" she protested.

"Relax," he said.

"Bastard!" Rehaan shouted.

Nikhil frowned and turned around. "He wasn't supposed to come so soon."

"What?!" She frowned, confused.

"He is early," Nikhil said.

"How dare you?" Rehaan shouted and fired another shot in the air.

"But if he has, let's deal with him," Nikhil said and faced Rehaan, shielding her.

"What?" she asked sounding like a parrot.

Rehaan pointed the gun at them.

"He was supposed to come after an hour, but he has always been impatient, hasn't he?" Nikhil said as if talking to himself.

"How do you know all this? How can you be so cool about all this!" she frowned, her eyes on Rehaan who was seething with fury.

"Wasn't this supposed to play out like this?" Nikhil asked. "The circle has to complete."

Before she could ask him not to speak in riddles, Rehaan shouted again, "Bastard, I'm going to kill you."

She tried to push Nikhil behind her, but he wouldn't let her.

"Have you gone mad, let me go and pacify him or he will kill you."

"He'll not kill me… or you either."

"Huh…?" Everything seemed so bizarre.

"He needs me alive for his holy war, and he will keep you alive for his ego. In both cases, we are going to be tortured."

"Then why did you come here?"

"Every moment spent together is bliss, isn't it?" Nikhil turned to look at her. "But we have one more option too."

"Option?"

"This." He held the silver charm she had given him.

And before she could react he put it in his mouth. He fell at her feet in a matter of seconds.

"No," she whispered, and her eyes snapped open.

It was pitch dark. The forest and sunshine disappeared, and she found herself in her cold, lumpy bed. Her heart still galloped, not in ecstasy but in fear from the nightmare. What a bizarre dream! She marveled at the imagination of her subconscious mind. But he had seemed so real. Just like his pictures, except for that scar on his cheek.

In the bed adjacent to her, *khala* muttered something softly and turned to the other side.

After her parents' death, Ayesha had schooled herself to go with the flow. But the last two weeks had made her yearn for something more. Forbidden desires clutched at her heart and refused to remove their tentacles. Getting through the day had become a burden. Her mind refused to stop thinking about him. Whenever she could lay a hand on anyone's phone, she searched for Vikram Seth to get a glimpse of Nikhil in the photographs. There had been no fresh news of his rescue or return. Obviously, it would have been hushed for his safety. She herself had suggested it.

Sometimes she regretted refusing his offer of running away with him. Then, she huffed. It was a fanciful idea, anyway. Rehaan would have never let her escape. His ego was bigger than the love he professed for her. He would have relentlessly pursued her till his last breath. And Nikhil would have gone back to his Esha.

She sighed. She wished she'd asked him about Esha, and been done with the nerve-wracking curiosity.

***

CHAPTER THIRTEEN

"I want to talk to Rao," Nikhil declared the moment Karan entered the apartment. It had been two days and he still hadn't been called for that talk Rao had promised. Having nothing to do, Nikhil felt caged up in the apartment. The days were boring, the nights full of nightmares.

"I'll pass on your request to him."

The bland statement uttered like he were an automaton irked Nikhil even more. "You are getting boring, pal, come up with a new line."

"You are behaving like royalty, dude. Get real." Karan stood before him with his hands crossed. "Rao is heading a department. Did you think he would be sitting on his ass, twiddling his thumbs, waiting for a chance to please you?"

"Quit coming up with smart answers, Karan. I know I am a civilian, but I am no imbecile. If I begin to put two and two together I will come up with the right answer, and your department will not even know what hit it."

"I don't know what your gripe is. I don't even know what you are talking about?"

"For one, I wonder why I'm getting the treatment generally accorded to a state witness. I also wonder why a field operative like you, the chosen one who was stationed at Pulwama to sniff out the terrorists, has suddenly been reduced to becoming my nanny."

Karan glared at him for a few seconds, then stormed toward his room.

Nikhil was satisfied that he had done enough to rattle the agent. That night sleep came easily, but so did the nightmares.

They all began in the basement.

He was tied to a crucifix in the center of the room and four faceless men sat around him, talking, laughing. The huge generator-like contraption sat in one corner with a gigantic red lever. No one touched the lever, nor were there any electric wire or probes attached to his body but still, he could feel the current running through him. And instead of pain, he felt a rush of both fear and revulsion through his veins, immobilizing him.

The laughter and conversation faded as Ayesha came down the stairs. Her long waist-length hair was spread over her shoulders and her nose-ring glinted despite the low light in the room. He opened his mouth to warn her to run away but no sound came out of his throat. She looked at him, then at his captors. The next second a silver hawk flew into the room and sat on her shoulder.

Silence reigned in the basement as everyone's gaze fell on her. To his surprise, the group stood up reverently—everyone moving in a pre-planned fashion. One of them stepped forward and handed her a gun. She moved toward Nikhil in a trance and examined each of his wounds.

"You didn't follow my instructions," she whispered.

He couldn't understand what she was talking about and tried to explain this to her, but couldn't make his tongue obey.

"I had told you to chew on the silver charm were you to get captured again. Why do I have to do everything?

Why should I pay the price for everything?" She placed the gun on his chest.

A dead calm settled in his heart. That was it. It was going to be over. If she killed him, no harm would come to her. But to his surprise before pulling the trigger she pulled the black thread on her neck, revealing the silver charm. A second one! Looking into his eyes, she placed the locket in her mouth.

"No, no, no!" he shouted and struggled against the ropes binding him.

"No!" The gun exploded. He lurched against the wooden shaft behind him. At the same time, she too fell down on the floor. The gun slipped out of her hand. The hawk flew away laughing like the man in *khakhi* cargos.

He sat up panting and found himself on the bed drenched in sweat. The only sound was the steady hum of the air-conditioner. The streetlight filtering through the curtains threw faint shadows in the room. Thankfully, he hadn't screamed out loud. It would have been embarrassing if Karan had heard.

He took a sip from the water bottle kept on the bedside table and fingered the charm on his neck. This was the first time she had featured in his nightmares. Her face, as he had seen that last night in Pulwama, appeared in his mind.

Something clicked.

He saw it in a flash, clear as a reflection in the clear water. The thing that had glinted that night when he had turned back toward her was the charm around her neck. A second charm, like the one she had given him.

She had worn another cyanide capsule around her neck. Why? The fact that she had two such mortal charms was quite baffling. Did they manufacture it for the masses? What did she have to fear, living as she did with relatives? Had she fed him a cock-and-bull story about migrating from PoK?

The feeling that had begun when he had left Ayesha intensified. There was something he was missing. Something vital. Things were not adding up. When they had been cornered by the two men in the forest, one had been gunned down by a man sent by Rao. She wasn't surprised. Had that man helped her all along during his rescue, right from the basement? Was Karan the same man? Why did Rao want to keep his escape hidden from his own parents and Vikram? What was the risk in their knowing? What forces were they up against?

He rubbed a hand over his eyes and hobbled to the window. All was quiet and peaceful outside in sharp contrast with his insides. The questions were driving him crazy. And his restricted movements frustrated him. He had to meet Rao. He needed information. He needed answers.

***

In his own room, Karan watched Nikhil settle down to sleep again on the live feed on his laptop. The camera covered the entire room except for the bathroom. Nikhil's nightmares often woke Karan up. The guy was suffering from PTSD.

The many days he had spent in captivity and the torture he had undergone had taken their toll on him. And now, living in isolation and not being able to meet his loved ones was making it worse. Karan was getting worried about Nikhil's condition.

***

"Come on, get ready," Karan said two days later at breakfast.

"What are you so excited about?"

"You wanted an audience with the boss, and you are getting it."

Nikhil was not surprised at the summons. Everything pointed to the conclusion he had arrived at, and Rao was not a fool to think that Nikhil was one.

Karan took Nikhil to a hotel in the hatchback. Rao was already present when they arrived at the designated room, sitting on the couch with a tea tray on the table in front of him. Rao didn't get up to greet him. As Nikhil made himself comfortable on the single-seater opposite Rao, Karan positioned himself near Rao's couch, leaning on the wall.

"Want some tea?" Rao asked.

"No, water is fine."

"I hear you are getting very restless and you even tried to bribe the maid to lend you her phone."

Nikhil raised his brows. "What do I have apart from my handsome face to bribe her with?" It was getting increasingly difficult to control his irritation.

"Karan says you were dying to meet me," Rao said.

"I thought you'd share with me the reason why I am under house arrest."

"You are not under house arrest. We are just trying to keep you safe."

"Why are you keeping me safe? Why do you give a damn?" Nikhil asked.

He didn't elaborate further so Nikhil decided to lay his cards down. "I have had lots of time to think."

"Okay." Rao sat back without taking his eyes off him. "So?"

"Ayesha is not who she says she is."

Rao's jaw tightened imperceptibly for a split second then he relaxed, but Nikhil noticed it and allowed himself a moment of satisfaction. He was right.

"She might not have had a chance to brief you as to how she orchestrated my escape. But I can tell you first-hand. I was there, and was very much aware of what was happening around me."

"I have never doubted your intelligence, Nikhil."

"Back in the Tral, I wondered how she was so cool about trekking through the forest. She seemed extremely confident about the topography in the wilderness. The only thing that scared her was the fear of being found out." Nikhil paused to study Rao's reaction. But after that first involuntary reaction, Rao sat as calm as a panther, his face betraying nothing, so Nikhil continued. "Why would she go to such lengths to save me?"

"No idea." Rao looked at the ashtray on the table, matter-of-factly as if he too was contemplating the same question. "Please carry on."

"In the forest when Karan shot that man—I am assuming it was Karan—and I slit the other man's throat, she was shocked because she knew one of the men, but she wasn't surprised at someone else being there to save us. It was almost like she knew that someone was there to protect her. And she gave me this." Nikhil took the charm out of his pocket and held it out for them to examine.

Rao squinted at the charm but didn't touch it.

"This is a cyanide capsule in a silver casing. She had another one too."

Rao shrugged.

Nikhil expelled a long breath. "Is she one of your agents?"

Rao looked at him like a wise owl watching a foolish mouse frolick.

"You know you can trust me," Nikhil added.

Rao smiled a little. "I know you can be trusted, Nikhil. And I know what you are capable of… yes. But the less said the better it is. Trust me. It's really quite unfortunate that you got embroiled in a thing which has far-reaching implications if anyone even gets a whiff of your escape."

"Unfortunate?" Nikhil stood up suddenly and winced. "You are comparing the torture that I went through in that room with bad luck?"

"Relax. Sit down and answer one of my questions honestly then I'll tell you whatever you want to know."

Nikhil sat down, scowling at him.

"The question is… what can you do if I tell you the truth?"

Nikhil's hands fisted. What should he say? That he wanted revenge. How filmy that would sound! And that he had fallen for that girl who had saved him? That he cared for her and wanted her to return safe and sound? That he didn't want that terrorist's hands on her?

Taking his silence as a tacit retreat, Rao ruthlessly pressed on. "What will happen if you know the complete story? They have marked you as their enemy. The less you know, the better it is."

"I want to be involved in the mission whenever the time comes. I have to get involved… I have to… I… I…" Unable to put his feelings into words, Nikhil stood up again and began to pace, forgetting the pain in his leg for once. "I want to tear that man limb from limb… the one who took my life from me… I want to… kill him."

Narrowing his eyes Rao looked at him. For a second Nikhil thought he would just laugh at his bravado and ask him to be practical, to forget everything and move on, but then he confirmed what Nikhil had suspected from the day a blue-eyed girl had rowed the boat across the lake.

"You are right. Ayesha is not who you think she is."

Karan straightened from the wall and let out a long breath as Rao continued. "They suspect there is an informer in their group and think he is supplying information to the authorities. Which is what Ayesha is doing."

"They think RAW is involved," Nikhil clarified remembering the cold, dark basement.

"It's a terrorist group, and for the past many years we are after their head of operations, Altaf Muhammad, Rehaan's uncle. When we had the opportunity to plant our agent in their household, we did that."

"How long has she been there with them?"

"Three years."

"She has been with those brutes for *three years!*" Nikhil was shocked.

"It wasn't meant to be three years. We had assumed it won't be more than a few months. But Altaf went into hiding after the attack on the Pulwama army cantonment and he's not surfaced for the last three years."

"And you let her remain there! Do you have any idea what she's going through?"

"We have always kept an eye on her. We have made sure she's safe."

"An eye on her! Can you see inside their house? Can you see what happens inside those walls?"

Rao looked a little taken aback. "We have our trusted people around her. Ayesha can call it off any time she wants. I have always made it clear to her that she can quit the moment she feels uncomfortable."

Nikhil looked at him with an angry smirk. "Looks like you greatly underestimate your agent's guts, Mr. Rao. Her guts and her commitment to your mission." Then unable to control himself, Nikhil said what he had been dying to say. "Do you have any idea of the kind of sexual harassment she is being subjected to by that nephew, Rehaan?"

For the first time, Rao dropped his eyes to his desk and picked up a pen. "Why do you presume that we have not thought of every eventuality?"

"Ah, yes. And this is the answer for every damn eventuality?" He threw the silver charm on the desk.

"Emotions do not rank high in our kind of work. She was doing fine till now, until you came along. This whole foolhardy rescue that she undertook could have seriously compromised her position, and we are trying to remedy that."

"And you not only gave her one but two!" Nikhil continued as if he hadn't heard Rao, but somewhere his mind registered that these men had been willing to let him die and that Ayesha had actually gone against her orders to rescue him. "What about if she gets married to that devil and still your mission is not successful? What if she gets pregnant?"

"You don't even know the stakes involved." Rao cut into his tirade calmly, but his steely tone indicated the extent of the liberty he had taken. "As I said, the fact that she helped you escape has put us in a bind. We can't take the risk of your going back to your life till the mission is over and she is back, or… she dies."

Nikhil hands fisted at the clinical way the last few words were uttered.

Rao continued as Nikhil stared furiously at him. "If you go back home, the media will go crazy and the terrorists will know your location. As long as Vikram continues to search for you, there is ambiguity about your survival. But if they know you are alive, they will definitely come after you. And Ayesha won't have any chance of survival."

Nikhil sat studying the old man, taking deep breaths, and pondering over the various scenarios. "What are my options?" he asked after a few moments.

"You remain in hiding till we kill them, or till Ayesha is no longer in the picture."

"How long will that take?"

"Two months, or two years. We are not sure. This job is mostly a waiting game."

"When did you come to know I was being held there?"

Rao had the grace to look guilty. "On the eighth day of your disappearance."

Nikhil pursed his lips. She had informed them the day he had told her his name and they hadn't done anything. Then she had taken it upon herself to rescue him. He stood up and limped toward the French window in the room. So angry was he with them that he wanted to smash something. No. He wanted to shoot Rao then and there.

"There was no option," Rao insisted. "We don't have a way to communicate anything back to her. There—"

"Spare me the details and… excuses."

"Rescuing you would have confirmed their suspicion that we indeed have an informer there. That again would have put her life in danger. As it is Rehaan doesn't even allow her to keep a phone. What if they had put her under house arrest? Then we wouldn't have had any means of contacting her."

The fact that his rescue could have put her life in danger calmed him down a bit.

"Nikhil—" Rao began.

"Who is she?" Nikhil turned around.

"I can't tell you that."

Nikhil took a deep breath. "I need to do this on my own. The safe house suffocates me."

"I'm afraid that's not an option."

"I promise I'll vanish from the face of the earth. You need not worry about that."

"I'm sorry."

"I'll take the identity you have created and be in touch with only Karan, but I have to be on my own. I can't have people breathing down my neck."

"Hey, I don't breathe down your anything!" Karan drawled.

Rao stared at Nikhil contemplating the odds.

"I have resources and know every trick of the trade, Rao." Nikhil pressed on. "No one will be able to trace me unless I wish them to. Believe me, I do not have any intention of getting captured again. And I have this, too." He picked up the charm from the table.

"I can agree on one condition. You need to get plastic surgery done, including facial changes. Nikhil Mahajan has to vanish for… forever. Nothing should connect you to the life that you had led before the bomb blast."

"Done," Nikhil agreed. He had come to the same conclusion, having thought through every scenario in the past week. "…and I want to be in on the mission for the final showdown."

"That's impossible, if they get—"

"They'll not recognize me. I want in whenever it happens. Else, I can go by myself. I'm capable of it once my leg heals, and you know that."

Rao thought about it then nodded.

"We can't let him go like this." Karan scowled spreading his hands.

Rao looked at Karan then glanced at Nikhil, who met his gaze unflinchingly.

"Do you need us to get you an identity?" Rao asked.

"I believe you already have that sorted?"

Rao nodded.

"I'm fine with Neal Mehra."

Rao handed him a paper with a phone number printed on it. "Memorize that number, then burn the paper. Stay in touch. Get fit soon. Remember, we might not have much time."

Nikhil nodded at Rao, then at Karan, and they left.

***

"How can you trust him like that?" Karan asked when he met Rao again after dropping Nikhil at the apartment.

"Do you know his friendship with Vikram Seth began when they were on a trek and Vikram saved his life?"

"Yes."

"He made himself Vikram's shadow after that… He hasn't verbalized it but it's the same sentiment which I see now for Ayesha… and something more."

"Do you think he's capable of keeping a lid on everything?"

"Oh, on that, I've no doubt."

***

CHAPTER FOURTEEN

Khala called the kazi that week and fixed the wedding date for a day roughly three months from then.

Up till then, Ayesha had felt safe under the watchful eyes of *khala*, because of her upright notions about Rehaan's conduct in society. But now she felt the noose tightening around her neck. Rehaan loved her, but he sometimes could get rough when *khala* wasn't looking. What would happen once he had complete control over her?

Life had begun to seem like a prison. A prison of her own choice. Everyone had asked her opinion and she had said yes. That was the plan. Revenge and duty drove her. But what if this didn't pan out the way she wanted?

That was the risk she and the higher-ups had never envisaged. They had never thought that Altaf Muhammad would manage his activities without even entering his hometown or his village. The people were so loyal to him and the cause that they had assumed he would feel safe there and visit often.

Perhaps he would come to the wedding. She had to wait. Again. Never mind. She would. Even if she had to get married in the process of waiting. As it was she didn't even consider it a real marriage. The event was just another step toward her goal. Rehaan was handsome and kept himself clean. What more could she ask for? Till now she had been resisting his attention. Maybe that was the reason he was so persistent. She would be nice to him and wait for her prey. Duty and the mission always came first.

***

Ayesha watched *khala* discuss the satins and brocades. Though she didn't like any, she agreed with every choice the old woman made. *Khala* wanted to impress her relatives and the neighbors. Whom did Ayesha have to impress? Her family was gone, her parents, dead. The only thing that drove her was her promise to her parents and her own survival. She wasn't interested in the clothes, but there was one thing she needed to buy which she would get only in the market. She got the chance soon.

"Ayesha, do you want to buy something?" *khala* asked magnanimously.

"A few knick-knacks," she said.

"We'll go to the market on the next *jumma*."

She nodded docilely.

Next Friday, as promised, *khala* took her to the market. Ayesha zeroed in on her favorite shop, which contained various knick-knacks for girls. To her alarm, Rehmaan *chacha*, the owner of the shop and a widower, was not present. His assistant was there, but she had to contact *chacha*. Where was he? He was supposed to give her the ring. He knew she always came on Fridays. She selected some baubles and rejected some, then rejected them all. Rehmaan *chacha* was her only contact for the job.

She wasn't sure what to do as the assistant kept showing her various earrings, *jhumkas* and bangles. Finally, she selected a set of bangles and a pair of *jhumkas*. She was paying for them when she heard the familiar voice.

"You should try this, Ayesha. Your blue one has lost its sheen." Rehmaan *chacha* was back, and he held a large ruby ring in his hand. The ruby, of course, was fake, but the ring was beautiful.

"Oh, this is exactly what I was looking for. It'll match my wedding dress too." She tried it on. It fit her ring finger perfectly. "How much is it?" This was the third time she was buying this kind of ring from him.

As she paid for her purchases, nobody noticed the piece of paper she slipped to him. She bid him farewell and joined *khala* at the grocery shop.

***

K. N. Rao sat staring at the translated and decoded the message.

'Wedding three months from today.'

There had been numerous occasions in the past three years when he received this kind of message but they had all been false alarms. This time though he was a bit more hopeful. It was a wedding after all.

He picked up his phone and called Karan.

***

A week later, Nikhil had a tearful reunion with his parents in the waiting room of the secretariat office in Delhi. Nikhil had arrived two hours earlier, entering through the second entry gate. His parents had come with Vikram, thinking they would get an update from the Home Ministry. They had been astounded to see him there.

His mother couldn't understand why he had to disappear again. It was difficult to explain the situation without telling them about the whirlpool he was trapped in. Vikram came to his rescue and calmed her down.

"You can't look happy ever, Ma," Nikhil told his mother, "You love putting on a tragedy act, don't you." He teased her as she wiped her tears. "You will have to give Nirupa Roy a run for her money now."

"Who can look happy when they can't visit their only son, or play with their grandchildren?" she said. "At least tell us how can we contact you?"

"You can't."

"Nikhil…" Tears appeared in her eyes and she broke down again.

"I'll come and visit you, whenever possible," he promised, hugging her hard.

After taking them back, Vikram arranged for a plastic surgeon in a private clinic abroad under a false name. Apart from removing the scars, Nikhil was given subtle changes to his nose and cheeks too. There were no records of the surgery.

Money definitely went a long way in getting things done discreetly in the world.

***

2 months later

Vikram sighed as he entered his farmhouse at Alibaug that weekend. Nothing was going as per plan, not in the business world nor in his personal life. He was worried about Nikhil and anxious about Esha's response.

"You look worried, buddy!" A familiar voice from the shadows of his bedroom had him pivoting around.

"Nick! How come…?"

"You better learn to call me Neal. I'm a new man."

"Let me look at you properly." Vikram raised his hands to the switchboard.

"Don't switch on the main lights."

"No, of course not, this is good enough." He switched on the night bulb. "You really look different, except for your eyes. They worked on the jaw too?"

"Yes."

"I can spy a few scars."

"They'll fade in a few months' time."

"How did you get inside?"

Nikhil chuckled. "Come on you shouldn't be asking this question! I designed the security system and the dogs know me."

"Ah… yes." He grinned, shaking his head. "So, how are you?" he asked once they sat down comfortably with a drink in hand.

"Great. I'll take off in a few hours. Just wanted to give you a glimpse of the new me. How is it going with Esha?" Nikhil asked.

"I'm having her followed." Vikram smiled.

Nikhil began to laugh. It was very rare for his friend to pursue a woman, generally, it was the other way around.

"What?" Vikram scowled.

"Why, in the name of the devil, are you having her followed?" Nikhil asked in between bouts of laughter.

"She is running from me. You know how busy I am. I fear she might go underground after her sister's wedding, she has already changed her number once. And I'm determined to bring her back into my life."

"You know her sixth sense, she might catch your men red-handed." Nikhil smiled.

"That's a possibility." Vikram chuckled, then looked at Nikhil. "So, what next?"

"I'm going to stay around Delhi. I've zeroed down on a studio apartment in the NCR. Have to be close by whenever they call me."

"Do you need money? What else can I do for you?"

"Nothing. You have done more than enough."

"I want you back."

Nikhil smirked. "I'm back."

"I meant your old, jovial self."

Nikhil stared at his glass.

"What's eating you up, Nick?" He placed his hand on Nikhil's. "What happened there?"

"You remember when you saved me on the mountains? I felt I was in your debt and taking care of your security gave me the satisfaction that I'm doing something to repay that debt. Now... there... in that village, someone saved my life again."

Vikram opened his mouth to say something, but couldn't form the words.

"I know, I haven't disclosed this to anyone," Nikhil continued. "She can't be exposed."

"She?"

"You know what this is?" Nikhil took out the black thread from his pocket.

"Seems like a *taveej*, a charm to ward off a curse."

"Yes, it seems like it, but it is not that. The silver encasing contains cyanide."

"What!" Vikram snatched it from his hand. "What are you doing with it?"

Nikhil chuckled. "Don't worry, I don't intend to take it. She gave it to me."

"Really, what kind of person saves your life and then gives you cyanide?"

"I wasn't in a shape to walk alone and since she could help me only during the night and had to leave me for at least twenty hours there was a risk of them finding me. She said it was better to end my life than to get captured."

Vikram narrowed his eyes but didn't say anything and waited for him to continue.

"The issue is not that she gave me the capsule, but when I was about to leave her to go to the army camp I saw another similar capsule on a thread around her neck. I can't get it out of my head. She saved me, but is she safe? As I sit here in complete comfort and safety, is she living and breathing? The thought doesn't let me sleep, Vikram."

"You want to talk to a doctor?"

Nikhil chuckled. "I'm not suffering from any trauma. I just want to go there and make sure that she is safe. Although I also feel like torturing that man in a worse way than he tortured me. Bastard! I want to rip him apart with my bare hands."

"That's not advisable." Vikram shook his head.

Nikhil chuckled. "I know you'll say think of a strategy rather than run headlong into a battle."

"Yeah… it works, almost always."

"So it does. I've learned to strategize from you, so I am not going to do anything that foolhardy."

Vikram knew him too well to protest and raised his glass in a toast.

Nikhil smiled. A smile that never reached his eyes.

***

Nikhil settled into the apartment in NCR, with the same routine every day. He would wake up at six a.m. and do exercises for strengthening his muscles. Then, for appearance's sake, he would get ready and pretend to go to work. Usually, his destination was the local library or a cyber café. Later in the evening, he would hit the gym.

In the library, he pored over real-life espionage books, and in the cyber café he played video games. Back at the apartment, he searched for anything and everything related to Rao on a secure, untraceable internet connection.

He had an inkling that everything began with Rao. He searched and searched, but couldn't find anything except the mundane details of school and college education, and how he had risen in the ranks to become the Principal Secretary in the State Department.

After that, there was almost no mention of anything about his induction into the field of intelligence. Nikhil expected that; he would have been disappointed if such information were readily available. It would have been a serious security lapse. Nikhil switched to his family, close friends, and acquaintances from college.

It took him ten days of relentless searching and applying all his hacking skills to come across a news item which he knew could be the key to all the answers he sought. The article carried news about the kidnapping and death of ACP Hussein Malik and his wife ten years ago. Though nothing in the report hinted at any connection to Rao, one of the funeral pictures carried the familiar figure standing solemnly in the background. Nikhil zoomed into the photograph and stared at the grainy, young version of Mr. K. N. Rao.

ACP Malik had been kidnapped by some unknown assailants and his wife gunned down during the skirmish. A few days later his body had been fished out from a lake. He had been tortured and had died due to the injuries inflicted. The police suspected the involvement of Altaf Muhammad the head of the then rising rebel militant group Jamat-e-Mujahideen in Kashmir. The only thing Nikhil couldn't fathom was how Ayesha fit into all this? Not that he expected he would find the information. Rao was good.

He searched for information on ACP Malik, but couldn't find anything. It was as if the person didn't exist in the virtual world. Nikhil had to contact Vikram once again to get the complete dossier on ACP Malik through his contacts.

He spent his days, waiting for information, exercising, and dreaming up various scenarios in which he would meet her again. It had become an obsession.

His doubts became reality when he read the information sent by Vikram.

The couple was survived by their daughter, Ziya, who had been around twelve at the time of the gruesome incident. If she was twelve or thirteen then, she would be twenty-two now. According to the details she had been sent to Canada for further studies after her parents' death.

No matter how hard he applied his hacking skills and resources, he couldn't find a latest picture of the daughter. The only one he could find was a black-and-white school photograph when she was admitted to a school in Srinagar at the age of nine.

There were numerous Ziya Malik's on the social media but none matched with Ayesha. Of course, the Ziya Malik he wanted might have a social media profile under a pseudo name, but he didn't have face recognition software to trace her. His intent behind the search was not only to satisfy his mental peace but also to gauge how foolproof Rao's privacy measures were. No one should be able to trace her, ever.

He sat staring at the screensaver which appeared after two minutes of inactivity and wondered what he would do if he found her recent, colored photograph? Would he find the same mesmerizing eyes looking at him? Were Ziya and Ayesha the same person? If so, how had she landed up in Altaf Muhammad's hometown? What if she was caught?

The image of the silver charm flashed in front of his eyes.

***

CHAPTER FIFTEEN

'Get ready.' The message came early that morning on Nikhil's unlisted number, known only to Karan and Vikram.

Nikhil rose from the floor where he had been doing his stretching exercises, part of his physiotherapy regime.

'??' Nikhil wrote.

'We have a date. Maybe this time we'll get the finale we have been waiting for all these years.'

'Maybe?'

'Yes. A couple of other times there have been false alarms. He was supposed to come but didn't.' Karan didn't elaborate and Nikhil didn't ask. He knew only about Altaf and that was enough.

'It could happen this time too?' Nikhil had not anticipated this scenario.

'This time we are hopeful. It's not every day his favorite nephew gets married.'

'Married?'

'Yes.'

'With her?'

'Who else?'

Nikhil didn't want to know more. From then on things happened at a fast pace. Karan met him at the shooting range for a few hours. He didn't comment on his looks as he had been the one to get his first passport-size photograph for preparing the identification papers.

Nikhil felt good to meet someone after living alone for weeks.

The gun felt heavy, yet familiar, in his hands. A strange calm had settled in his heart, now that he was involved in the action. The recoil of the gun jolted his hand, but after a few shots, the academy training kicked-in and his hands were steady.

"How will we take her out from there?" he asked one day at the shooting range.

"We have to fake her death."

"How?"

"The same way they did yours."

Nikhil frowned.

Karan continued, "Don't worry. As far as I know them, I don't think they will bother with a DNA test of an insignificant girl."

They traveled by public transport as journalists. Not that anyone asked but that was the identification they carried. Karan already had a room rented in his name in Pulwama. They settled in the cheap one-bedroom apartment. Karan, having done this sort of thing many times, soon assembled the surveillance equipment and arranged a two-wheeler, which was extremely handy for small errands and in navigating the hilly roads of the small town.

Everything was set in a few days and then the wait began.

"I wonder how she landed up in that family?" Nikhil asked Karan one evening, not sure if he would answer him.

"Who?"

"ACP Malik's daughter Ziya, aka Ayesha." Nikhil shot in the dark, but Karan's reaction told him all he needed to know.

"How did you even get that information?" Karan demanded.

"I can put two and two together."

Karan stared at him, worry etched on his handsome features.

"Don't worry, I connected this through Rao. No one else will be able to."

"Still!" Karan wasn't happy.

"Take down Rao's photo at ACP Malik's funeral from the internet. There's only one." Nikhil said, as Karan furiously typed on his phone.

"Which site?" Karan asked.

Nikhil gave him the information and repeated his question. "So how did she land up in that house?"

Karan hit the send button on the mobile and lifted his head. "Since the day her father's body was found, she wanted to go into intelligence. Rao dissuaded her as much as he could but had to give in when she threatened to commit suicide if he didn't let her contribute in some way."

"She didn't!"

"She did. I was there."

"She threatened that old codger, very brave of her." Nikhil smiled, all the more proud of her.

"Okay, so he agreed on the condition that she will have to complete her education and learn hacking and computers so that she could work in IT espionage. It was a safe and sound position. But as it happened, we came across the family of *khala's* sister, twice removed, who was migrating from PoK. They died in crossfire while illegally crossing the border. Their daughter, Ayesha, was sixteen. Everyone was dead. Ziya took the place of the daughter."

"But Ziya Malik was not sixteen at that time."

"No, she was nineteen, but her petite frame resembled the dead girl a lot. So, she pretended to be sixteen."

"And she landed at Altaf's brother's home."

"Yeah… since her parents had died, she could afford to remain quiet and withdrawn and learn their ways. She is already a Kashmiri, so learning a few new things was not very difficult. And they hadn't seen Ayesha for quite a few years. So, we got lucky."

"And you trained her in the other aspects?"

"Yes, we had only a few weeks. She is a quick learner and her thirst for revenge drove her, making my job easier."

Nikhil fell silent, contemplating over what he had been told. His respect for Ayesha no, Ziya, increased every time he learned something new about her.

***

On the eve of the wedding, Karan suited up calmly. Nikhil was already in a standard army uniform, which was a bit loose for him so he tucked it securely in the waistband and the boots, then checked his guns. The pair of night goggles, procured through private sources and a bit more high-tech than the standard army-issued ones, were tucked inside their bullet-proof vests. Over their uniforms and weapons, they pulled on grey, oversized *phirans* and caps.

As dusk turned into wintery night, they took the two-wheeler to the forest edge and parked it near a picnic spot. The small truck was already parked there with the keys taped under the chassis on the driver's side. They took out the body-bag from the back, arranged by Rao from the nearby morgue. Inside was a dead body of a girl matching Ayesha's height and frame.

They secured the truck and began the laborious trek into the forest toward the lake which bordered Rehaan Muhammad's backyard. The same path that Ayesha had taken to rescue him some four months back. It was a slow trek with Nikhil lugging the body-bag and Karan carrying the arms and other equipment, alternately.

Upon reaching the lake they uncovered the *shikara* kept upside-down under a bush and dragged it toward the lake. In a few minutes, they crossed the lake and hid the *shikara* in the old man's shed.

Having played his role to watch over Ayesha, the old man had been asked to go to the other village for the day, to keep him safe from the carnage.

Hiding in the woods, they did the recce of the house now visible because of the twinkling fairy lights which decorated it for the wedding. Though Karan thought there might not be a need for them to be involved in the actual encounter, Nikhil had his doubts. According to Karan, the army would do the job clinically; they had done this countless times in drills and in real situations.

No peace-loving civilian would be hurt. But Karan did not know the man who had interrogated Nikhil. The man with the hawk emblem on his cargos.

***

Ayesha sat in her room, dressed in the wedding ensemble, waiting. If everything went as per plan she would be free of the nightmare she had lived for the past three years. If not, she would have to wait for another day. But everything was worth it. She wanted to see fear etched into their eyes. Fear for their lives. Fear of death.

The faint notes of *shehnai* hit her ears, but she longed to hear the name she had been briefed about. She fingered her new ring. The fake ruby winked at her twinkling in the colored lights hanging on the window. She had bought something like this so many times and every time she had had no reason to use it. Would she finally be able to use it tonight?

She prayed with all the fervor in her heart for the ordeal to end. To be honest, she was scared of Rehaan but had never voiced her fear into the right ears. Krishnan uncle had assured her she only had to transmit a coded message via their standard mode of communication and he would send a team to get her out.

But, of course, getting her out also meant aborting the mission. That was never an option. And that was why she had endured these years in this hellhole. Rehaan was the only key to bring the mouse out of his burrow. She would not let Uncle Krishnan or herself down. She had made a promise to herself and Altaf's arrest or death was the culmination of everything they had planned.

Shabnam smiled as she came in, pulling her out of her reverie.

"It's time," she whispered, pulling the red *dupatta* over Ayesha's face and covering her till her chest.

The progress to the hall was slow thanks to her heavy *sharara*, the hem sweeping the floor, which she had to lift a bit to be able to walk. Shabnam helped her sit on the low wooden platform where all the ladies sat surrounding her. A fine, translucent, satin curtain separated them from the men in the outer hall. *Khala* fussed around her, waving a hundred-rupee note around her and handing it over to the maid who swept the outer corridors of the house.

Behind the security of her veil, without lifting her head, she scanned the scene beyond the curtain. Rehaan sat happy and resplendent in his golden *sherwani*. Even she couldn't deny that he was a handsome man. Slowly her eyes scrutinized each and every face in the room. She could spot Shehzaad deep in conversation with another man she couldn't recognize, a couple of Rehaan's friends stood in one corner, then there were the neighbors and Shabnam's father. But her eyes couldn't spot the face that had haunted her from the day he had snatched her childhood in one shot.

There was still time. He might show up during the dinner or at least for the ritual when the elders blessed the newlyweds. A sudden hush fell in the hall and her heart began to hammer as her eyes latched on to the door. But it was only the *kazi* entering the house. She turned away, deflated.

There was a shuffle of papers and the murmur of the *dua* being offered to God Almighty. She fingered the ring and prayed she could use it soon. The *kazi* came to the dais where she sat and recited the usual words she had heard during the numerous weddings she had attended. Except, this time, it was her own wedding. And then she was asked the question. When she didn't answer, everyone thought she was being shy. The girls giggled and the older women nodded their heads in approval at her showing the proper restraint. The *kazi* repeated the question again. Shabnam nudged her elbow.

"*Kubool hai*," she whispered giving her consent to be wedded, then repeated the hated words two more times at the *kazi's* prompt.

A cheer erupted amongst the women and the men smiled clapping Rehaan on the back in congratulations. *Khala* kissed Ayesha's temple and waved another hundred-rupee note over her and handed it to a nearby maid. Now Ayesha knew why she had always complained about lack of money whenever she had to spend anything on Ayesha; she had been saving for this day, for her son and showing off their status in the village.

Rehaan too was asked for his consent by the *kazi*, which he gave with considerable enthusiasm. Then the feast began and the celebration continued late in the night.

A heaped plate of food was brought to Ayesha too, but she couldn't eat beyond a morsel or two. Shabnam and Asma kept teasing her and coaxing her to eat. Their constant chatter was getting on Ayesha's nerves but she tolerated everything, seeking only that one face that had haunted her since that ill-fated afternoon almost ten years back. A smiling face that had taken credit for her parents' murder. The face which had sent her into deep, guilt-ridden depression, until she had found her mission.

The mission which would prove to be his end. A mission to wipe that smile off his face. In fact, she wanted to squeeze the very life out of him. But where was he? Today was a big day. She had been sure his nephew's wedding would bring him out of his burrow in PoK.

Someone sat down beside her and giggled. Ayesha turned to find Asma in some secret conversation with another girl from the neighborhood. Silly girls. They were such simpletons. Ayesha dismissed them with an irritated shake of her head and resumed her vigil. The thin veil covering her head and face was a boon. She could freely scan the crowd without attracting any unwanted attention.

Soon the guests began to leave one by one, and her simmering rage slowly changed into desperation. Rehaan was already casting meaningful glances toward her, which she ignored under the garb of shyness. *Khala* was also showing signs of fatigue, and she bid goodbyes to the local guests enthusiastically. But she too was grumbling about Rehaan's uncle not showing up.

When only a handful of relatives were left yawning in various corners of the courtyard, Shabnam nudged Ayesha. "*Chalo ji, dulhan begam.* Time to go into 'the' room."

"Don't call me a bride," Ayesha finally snapped.

"Then what should I call you, *dulhan begam?*" Shabnam giggled. "I know you are scared," she muttered pulling her arm. "But why? I refuse to believe that Rehaan *bhai* has not kissed you even once."

"Shut up," Ayesha hissed, still glancing at the door.

"Don't be nervous, everything will be fine after the first night," Shabnam whispered.

"From where do you get all this information?" Ayesha scowled. "From your fiancé?"

"Maybe. I have many sources." Shabnam winked, completely unembarrassed.

The headache that had been brewing since the beginning of the day was by now nearly splitting her head. Ayesha didn't have the energy to prolong the hateful conversation, so she allowed Shabnam to take her to Rehaan's room. The sweet smell of the roses strewn across the marital bed made her want to retch. Roses were Rehaan's favorite flowers, associated with all the times he had tried to make unwanted advances on her, and so she had begun to dislike them.

Giggling and whispering suggestive comments Shabnam finally left the room. Ayesha's ears still tuned to the sounds from outside, awaiting *khala's* or Rehaan's excited greeting for their only close relative. But all her hopes died when Rehaan came inside and closed the door. Her hand clasped the new ring, then let go. She'd have to wait for another chance. There would be another chance and she'd wait for it. She sighed and forced a smile as Rehaan sat on the bed and held her hand.

"*Shukriya, jaan,*" he thanked her as he toyed with her fingers.

For what? For marrying him? He seemed to be in a generous mood and was probably drunk.

She looked at him and glimpsed the shadow of the villain of her life. But she would surrender herself. She had to, for the greater good. It was nothing big. People had sacrificed much more for causes they believed in. She had thought about this scenario many times by now and had reconciled to the eventuality. Now it was time to put her resolve to the test.

***

Karan and Nikhil watched the caterers wind up their work and go off to their respective homes, leaving the oven warm in a small tent set up along the wall outside the house. After thirty minutes of waiting and watching for any movement in the house and tent, they walked leisurely toward the tent carrying their bags. The presence of a man and a small boy, sleeping in the tent, didn't surprise Karan. He gestured to Nikhil and both took out a cotton wad tucked in their back pocket and placed them on the noses of the two. They would be out cold for at least six hours, enough time for Karan and Nikhil to disappear if there was no action. They then settled near the warmth of the oven for the signal.

No one except the army commander-in-charge of this raid knew about their presence. And even he didn't have the complete information but had agreed to the plan as the authorization had come directly from the Prime Minister.

***

Rehaan had taken off her *dupatta.* She closed her eyes as he came nearer, his breath fanning her cheeks. He smelled of local perfume as well as alcohol, nothing revolting, but still unpleasant. Cupping her face, he nuzzled her cheek, then kissed her lips. Her heart hammered with fear of the unknown.

"Ayesha, you are so lovely," he whispered, trailing his lips over her jawline and neck, as his hands went to the buttons of her *kurta.*

Ayesha jumped as she heard *khala* squeal and call out Rehaan's name at the top of her lungs. Instinctively, she knew that *he* had arrived. Her heartbeats switched to a different rhythm.

"What the—" Rehaan cursed under his breath. Muttering all kinds of expletives, he buttoned his *sherwani* and went out of the door.

Ayesha quickly straightened her *kurta,* arranged the *dupatta* around her head and rushed to the window opening into the corridor, but couldn't see anything. They had moved to the farthest corner of the main hall. What now? Would they call her to take his blessings? Her hand caressed the ring. She had to be absolutely sure before taking the next step.

As she had expected, Shabnam entered the room donning her *dupatta* and muttering under her breath. She looked like she had been woken up from sleep too. "*Chalo, dulhan begam. Chacha* is calling you."

At last.

Ayesha walked behind Shabnam with her head down. A few elder relatives sat surrounding the late-night visitor. Rehaan and Shehzaad stood like sentries behind him. Shabnam made her sit on the wooden *takht* where *khala* sat, and stood near it, chewing the corner of her *dupatta.*

"*Lo,* here is Rehaan's *dulhan.*"

"*Mubarak ho, mubarak ho,*" the visitor congratulated *Khala,* and held out a pouch toward Ayesha.

Khala nudged her with her elbow. Ayesha lifted her eyes and saw the man she had been waiting for the past three years. No, no… ten years. Altaf Muhammad.

Ayesha hoped no one noticed the surprise in her eyes as she dropped her gaze back to her hands. He was a frail man and did not look fearsome as his reputation had suggested. On the contrary, he looked old, like any ordinary mortal who had aged before his time. Ayesha took the pouch and hid her hands again in the voluminous folds of her wedding attire.

Under the *dupatta*, her fingers sought the ring on her left hand and she twisted the fake ruby stone studded into the ring a full circle, clockwise.

***

CHAPTER SIXTEEN

The beep from Karan's watch jolted him out of his thoughts, and Nikhil from the floor near the wall where he sat patiently, drilling a hole in the wall with a knife. Karan dialed a number on his mobile and disconnected after two rings. In a few minutes, the mobile and internet communication network ceased to work.

At the back of Rehaan's house, in the small hut opposite to where Karan and Nikhil hid, four men shed their *phirans* to reveal their army uniforms. They checked their weapons and equipment, as they waited for further instructions.

Two men near the mosque walked toward the cluster of houses uphill, where Rehaan's house was situated.

From the Indian army brigade headquarters, two trucks full of soldiers began their journey toward the target village in Pulwama district.

***

Ayesha looked at the watch Rehaan wore. From the position of the needles, she could make out it was around 2:15 a.m. It had been thirty minutes since she had initiated the signal. Though she didn't know the next course of action, all her nerves were on high alert. Krishnan uncle had said she would be rescued, but she didn't know when and how.

"*Allah taala ka shukra hai,*" *khala* was thanking God that everything had gone smoothly.

Everybody nodded in unison. Altaf and the other men who had come with him were served dinner. The entire household was present to get a glimpse of their leader and crusader.

'*The murderer.*' Ayesha dropped her gaze to her lap as years of hatred surged in her whole being.

To her chagrin and alarm, nothing happened even after half an hour when everyone began to retire again for the remainder of the night. Cots and blankets were arranged for the men in the corridor. *Khala* asked Shabnam and the other girls to escort Ayesha back to the room. Rehaan loitered around to make sure the visitors were comfortable.

Ayesha again sat in the room, her nerves taut with tension. Where were they? Did her ring work or not? In her agitation, she twisted the stone again. She was tired of the whole waiting game. Waiting for Altaf to appear. Waiting for the action to begin. Waiting to go back home to her job, her friends, to the memorabilia she had left behind with her landlord. Had it all been for nothing? Disappointment cloaked her so much that she even rued the day she had insisted on being included in the mission. She had even threatened Krishnan Uncle with suicide if he refused.

The next second, she was ashamed of her thoughts. All through her training sessions with her mentor, she had been warned about the drudgery, patience, and sacrifice required for the task. She remembered the day of her parents' funeral and her heart swelled with renewed energy.

She stood up to change her clothes and froze when the outer yard was suddenly lit up as if someone had switched on a massive torch in the sky. Someone shouted.

There was a loud clattering noise as if someone had kicked the used utensils kept near the tap in the courtyard in surprise. Then she heard the booming voice.

"All residents of the house of Rehaan Muhammad…" The voice of a local village elder boomed from the loudspeaker. "This is an official army search, please leave the house one by one from the main door. Anyone coming out of any other entrance will be shot."

'Yah, Allah! It's happening.' She ran to the door, but before she could open the door, there was a loud bang and someone screamed. Rehaan stormed into the room almost knocking her to the floor. Shehzaad too followed him in. She shrank back into the shadows behind the door.

The voice came again on the loudspeaker repeating the same message.

"Ayesha, find *ammi* and stay with her," Rehaan shouted rummaging in the big trunk, throwing all the clothes on the floor. He then took out a few bullet-proof vests and a couple of AK-47s.

"Wait a second, do you have the gun I gave you?"

She nodded.

"Take that and stay with *ammi*."

Ayesha spared a last look at the duo who were donning the vests, pulled her *dupatta* over her head and moved out of the room. The lights inside the house had all been switched off. But, there was enough light from the spotlights the army had arrayed outside to see clearly.

There were around fifteen to twenty relatives who stood in the corridor ready to move out. Most of the women were crying, but not *khala*. She sat on the wooden *takht,* surrounded by the clan. The women were trying to convince her to leave the house, but she stoically remained on the wide, wooden bench. Ayesha hoped her own face showed sufficient fear and gloom as she rushed toward *khala*.

"*Khala,* what's happening? What will we do?" she wailed behind the veil.

"Be quiet and stay with me." She caught hold of Ayesha in a vice-like grip and pulled her beside her on the *takht*. She held a pistol in the other hand.

Ayesha suddenly realized that *khala* was scared to the bones. Her hands trembled, and her voice shook as she shouted at others, urging everyone to follow the instructions being relayed on the loudspeaker.

Altaf was not to be seen anywhere, but his cronies had their vests on and their guns at the ready. Two of them took their positions near the windows facing the front door. Shehzaad and Rehaan peeped out of the back door. The backyard was also lit up with bright floodlights.

"There is a *shikara,* they can escape crossing the lake," *Khala* muttered. "If they can reach the *shikara*. Only if…"

"But they are there too, in the backyard," Ayesha said. "What will we do, *khala*? Are we not going?" she asked when she saw the women going out of the main door with their hands raised above their heads. Shabnam threw a glance at her before following her mother out.

"*Khala?*" Panic had her looking at *khala* and then at the shortening line of relatives leaving the house.

"Keep quiet, girl." *Khala* tugged at her hand painfully. "We are not going out till Rehaan is safe."

The old woman had gone mad. She was going to sacrifice both of them. What if they bombed the house? One by one people filed out of the main entrance, but *khala* sat determinedly on the *takht* in the corridor not letting Ayesha move from her side. Ayesha knew she was capable of shooting her if she dared to defy her.

***

Nikhil and Karan could only guess at what was going on. Karan's watch showed Ayesha's location and it appeared that only a wall separated them from her.

The hole in the wall was now the size of the muzzle of Karan's sniper rifle.

Karan peered from a small, uneven tear in the tent. He could see four army soldiers in position behind the trees just ten to twelve yards ahead of them, covering the back exit.

"She has been trained by the best, don't worry about her," Karan said when he saw Nikhil sitting still near the wall staring at the hole. Karan himself was mentally sifting through the plans they had discussed three years back. Would she remember plan B and had she done the preparation or plan C where she was supposed to pretend to be dead?

"What do you think of this?" Nikhil asked.

Karan looked at the ten-inch deep hole, one foot above the ground. According to the topography of the house, just one nudge to the brittle cement would allow them to look inside the central courtyard of the house.

"What if they notice it?" Nikhil whispered.

"Will they? In this chaos."

"How many do you think there are?"

"Two in the front, two or three on the roof covering the back, and three inside, apart from the women."

A loud clang jolted them out of their thoughts and their hands went to their guns inside their *phiran.*

Someone from inside had blasted one of the two floodlights at the back. The soldiers responded. Taking advantage of the noise from the firing guns, Nikhil hammered at the wall, and the brick and cement gave way to the view inside the house. The army continued to fire at the house to prevent the occupants from having another chance to blow the second floodlight, which was now the only means to see. But the terrorists did not relent and someone fired at the second light too. The area was plunged into darkness. Nikhil and Karan took off their *phirans* and put on their night goggles.

The bullet had come from the roof. One of the soldiers fired on the roof and they heard a scream and a thump. More soldiers rushed toward the backyard.

"One down, six left," Karan said, his eyes on his watch. His only focus was on his pupil, whom he had trained and who had made him proud today. They were about to nab the decade's most-wanted man tonight.

***

Ayesha sat alongside *khala* her hand numb as the older woman refused to loosen her grip. Rehaan and Shehzaad were positioned at the back windows and were relentlessly firing. Out of the four men who had come with Altaf, two were stationed at the front and two on the roof covering the back. He himself was running from one end to other shouting instructions and encouragement. They had been able to take out the floodlights at the back.

Altaf shouted for Rehaan. "Can we cross the lake?"

"There is an old *shikara*," Rehaan said. "But soldiers are swarming all around."

The other man stationed at the back shouted, "Abu is dead, shot on the roof." He then ran back to his position.

Altaf looked around and spotted *khala* and Ayesha. The hard gleam in his eyes chilled Ayesha to her soul. She could now see the beast inside him.

"Bhabhijaan, Allah ke naam pe shaheed hone ka din hai, tum tayyar ho?"

Ayesha's eyes widened in fear as he asked for the supreme sacrifice from *khala*. How could he? But *khala* nodded. *"Iss jihad mein hamari jaan bhi hazir hai, bhaijaan,"* she said and stood beside him, pulling Ayesha along with her.

The hateful man nodded at Shehzaad, who caught hold of Ayesha and pulled her to his side.

"Rehaan!" Ayesha couldn't help but look at him, unable to reach the gun which was in her purse hanging on her left wrist.

"What are you doing, Shehzaad *bhai*?" Rehaan asked as confused and terrified as Ayesha herself.

"Rehaan, our lives are more important to this war than the women's. We will take them as our shield and escape."

"No!" He stepped forward to pull Ayesha to his side.

"*Jihad* is supreme. You will always be remembered for this sacrifice, Rehaan," Altaf said. "Remember the oath that you had taken," he snapped when Rehaan didn't back down.

"Rehaan, stand back and save yourself," *khala* screamed at him.

A worried Rehaan looked at his mother then at Ayesha, conflicted between his duty and love, but he didn't step back. For the first time in three years, Ayesha felt a wee bit of sympathy for Rehaan—a person who had been caught in the whirlwind of his parental legacy. Altaf whispered something to Shehzaad, who lifted his gun.

***

Karan trained his rifle's monocular to the scene inside. People frantically moved at the far end of the corridor. One of the pillars obstructed his view. There was an argument going on in Kashmiri, which he couldn't hear clearly. His grip on the device tightened when a girl dressed in a bridal ensemble came into the view. She was being pulled by a tall man in the *khakhi* pants toward the back door and a man, not in his line of vision, was protesting.

Everyone moved forward in the courtyard giving him a clear view of the scene. Recognizing Altaf raised Karan's pulse. He could take him down then and there, but the hole had to be widened for both rifle and the viewfinder.

Judging by the clothes they wore, the person protesting must be the groom, Rehaan. Altaf was holding the old woman and the other tall man held Ayesha in a vice-like grip. They wanted to escape using the women as shields! Didn't they realize everyone would be killed?!

All of them were dead the moment they stepped out of the house with their guns. He had to take the men down inside the house.

"Give me the knife!" he hissed, putting the monocular aside.

"What's happening?" Nikhil asked urgently, leaning beside him.

"Have to widen the hole. Need a clear shot."

A shot rang out and a woman screamed, causing Nikhil to put his eye to the opening. The old woman was screaming and struggling against her captor. The man in the *sherwani* he had known as Rehaan, lay on the floor.

"Who is down?" Karan asked. "Are they killing their own?"

"Seems like it."

"Two down, five left."

"Karan, the man has a gun to Ayesha's head," Nikhil hissed.

"I know, hang on."

Karan and he worked frantically on the opening without making noise and making sure the dust fell on their side. The old woman was now screaming all kinds of profanity at the men.

"Shall I go on the roof?" Nikhil asked.

"No, the army might shoot you. Visibility is low."

A few heart-stopping minutes passed, and Karan finally positioned the rifle into the opening. Nikhil paced the tent.

"Stand down or you might get hit by a stray bullet," Karan said, his eyes trained on the scene inside.

Inside the tent, the older man had begun to stir. Nikhil hit him with the butt of his gun in frustration. The man lay limp on the floor, unconscious once again. Nikhil tied him and the younger lad with the ropes they had brought with them and stuffed pieces of clothes lying on the floor into their mouths.

"Stand down," Karan ordered and fired.

Nikhil and he lay flat on the floor as the wall was bombarded with retaliatory fire from the men inside. The next second there was a loud blast, and they covered their heads. A second later the wall that had shielded them collapsed all around.

***

Ayesha stopped struggling when Altaf fell clutching his stomach. Blood oozed out between his fingers, his clothes slowly turning red.

Somewhere in the distance, Shehzaad fired and shouted. A bomb exploded, and a wall collapsed. Dirt and debris rained down all around her, but she couldn't take her eyes off the man who lay three feet from her struggling for air and life. *Khala's* violent mourning penetrated the haze in her mind as she looked around.

Shehzaad pulled her along, relentlessly firing at someone to their left. He had bombed the left side of the courtyard. Boulders, dirt, and smoke obscured the view in that direction.

A wooden log fell on Altaf, who groaned again. Her attention snapped back to him. His eyes were red with pain and fear. She remembered her mother and father on that fateful funeral day as she watched her arch enemy take his last breath. With a long sigh, he died just a few feet from her.

Mission was accomplished, but she felt no sense of achievement. The past still remained the same—lonely and stark. She was drained, yet self-preservation kicked in. She looked around.

As far as she knew only three men were left—Shehzaad, one on the roof, and the one shooting in the front. She had been able to loosen the strings of her purse. If only she could reach her gun, she could take down the man who might take Altaf's position. She twisted her left hand to put it inside the purse, but it slipped off from her wrist. Amongst all the chaos, *khala* continued to scream and cry beside Rehaan's body.

Ayesha tried to see beyond the dirt and hoped someone would come and give her a chance at escape. Another scream was heard and someone fell to the floor. The roof was unguarded. She could hear soldiers shouting in the backyard.

"Stop that noise, for the love of *Allah*," Shehzaad shouted, and shot *khala*.

Ayesha shuddered and her breath hitched as *khala* rolled over Rehaan's prone figure. Shehzaad pulled her toward the broken wall, his attention and gun aimed at anyone who would appear in the opening. As they reached the wall, the whole structure of the house shuddered and collapsed on them.

***

Karan and Nikhil rushed inside the house, just as the roof collapsed. The debris and dust made it impossible to see

171

even with dawn breaking and the front floodlights on. A man lay dead just inside the collapsed back door. They couldn't see anyone else. Where was she?

Nikhil longed to call out her name, but couldn't take the risk. As they made their way inside, they heard someone cough and groan. Nikhil rushed toward the left, but broken wooden pillars blocked the path. Someone groaned again. Karan and he lifted the beams out of the way one by one. He saw a man, his hand twisted at an awkward angle but still holding an AK-47, lying dead under the *almirah* which had crashed over him. Karan kicked the gun away and moved ahead. The sight that lay before them chilled Nikhil to the core. A man and Ayesha were trapped under debris and the door frame which had collapsed over them.

They couldn't see Ayesha but could hear her calling out for help.

"Hang on, she'll be okay," Karan whispered restraining Nikhil's mad rush to reach her.

Slowly they cleared the space and hefted the frame off the two of them.

The man groaned and opened his eyes. Something in his voice caught Nikhil's attention. Silver glinted in the dark. Then he saw the dust-covered emblem on his cargo pants. The horrors of the basement came rushing to his mind. The hum of the generator and the smell of burnt flesh. Nikhil lifted his gun, looked straight into the man's eyes, and pulled the trigger.

Ayesha cringed and groaned again.

"Hey, it's me, shorty. Be still," Karan said and turned Ayesha gently. She looked dazed.

Nikhil sucked in his breath when he saw her bruises caked with dirt.

"Are you hurt? Can you move your limbs?" Karan whispered.

She nodded.

"Move carefully." He held her shoulders.

She moved her legs and arms slowly.

"Everything seems to be fine," Karan said, supporting her up.

She smiled at Karan, then looked at Nikhil. Confusion replaced the smile. As recognition dawned, she looked questioningly at Karan.

"Quickly, change your clothes." Ignoring the undercurrents, Karan handed her a bag. "And take off your jewelry, especially the nose ring. Not the ring. Yours has the transmitter. She already has a normal, fake ring."

They ran back to the caterer's tent and brought the dead body dressed in a bride's ensemble.

Ayesha unwrapped the *dupatta* and gave it to Karan, not acknowledging Nikhil at all. She wore the uniform over her clothes and knotted her hair and covered it with the army cap. Karan handed her a gun to complete the look of a soldier.

"What about these?" She held up her henna-patterned hands.

"Here, take these." Nikhil handed her his gloves.

She hesitated a few seconds before slipping them on. They were large for her hands but served the purpose of hiding the red pattern.

Hastily Nikhil put the nose ring, bangles and her *dupatta* on the body, while Karan planted a bomb near it. Casting a last look at the scene, Karan nodded and the three of them went out of the house. The Army was swarming around the outer periphery when the bomb exploded.

Guns in hand, Nikhil, Ayesha and Karan jogged to the last vehicle with army plates beyond the cordoned-off area. The commander nodded at them once, waving them forward. Nikhil took the wheel, while Karan sat back with Ayesha, keeping an eye if anyone followed them.

Nikhil drove the SUV at a steady pace on the road leading to the army cantonment. As they exited the village the road forked into the main highway and a narrow side road leading to another town. He took the side road. Their galloping heartbeats steadied as they traveled kilometer after kilometer away from Rehaan's house.

Driving the vehicle, Nikhil couldn't help but glance at the rearview mirror. She sat on the side bench with her arms crossed and her face bent down. Dirt clung to the bruise on her cheek. He wanted to hide her in his arms, shield her from the strife and trauma. She had recognized him. So fast. And he had been so proud of his disguise with his beard and all.

The white bullet-proof car at a distance brought him out of his musings. He stopped the SUV behind the car. Karan helped her get down their vehicle and escorted her to the car. Nikhil desperately wished to be with her, but the danger still lurked. Ayesha Khan was dead and Ziya Malik was in Canada. And he was supposed to be dead or missing.

'*Can it get any more complicated?*'

She stopped as Karan pulled open the door and turned to look at Nikhil. For a moment Nikhil thought she would come to him, but the next second she turned back and sat in the car. Once again he felt his soul getting ripped apart as she vanished from his sight. Karan closed the door of the vehicle, which left immediately with Rao at the wheel.

Karan joined him in the front of the SUV. "You okay?"

Taking a long breath, Nikhil nodded.

"Was he the one?" Karan asked.

Nikhil knew whom he was referring to. He nodded again.

Karan sighed. "Let's go. It's curtains now."

***

After Karan completed the formality of returning the car to the army office and closing the room in Pulwama, they took the first bus to Jammu, from where they flew back to New Delhi.

The first thing which Nikhil did when he got back to his lodging was to dial the unlisted number Rao had given.

"Where is she now?" he asked the moment Rao picked up the phone.

"I'm sorry. Can't tell you that."

"Why the hell not?"

"I don't want you to have any association with her."

"Even now? They are all dead."

"Not all, they are never dead. You'll never know. Once on their hit list, you are always on their list. It will be better if you forgot the whole affair." Rao disconnected the phone.

***

CHAPTER SEVENTEEN

It had been three months.

Ziya entered her apartment late that Tuesday evening. The day had been hectic at the university. Placing the takeout dinner on the kitchen counter, she switched on her laptop and hooked on the video camera application to watch the entrances. The live feed came on for the three doors—the main entry downstairs, her apartment door and the back exit—as she poured herself a glass of ice-wine, her favorite.

She had been lucky to get the same apartment in Canada, which she had vacated three years ago. The landlord had been very helpful in agreeing to store her memorabilia for so many years. She was also fortunate to have been allowed to continue the degree course she had left midway. Uncle Krishnan had pulled some strings, of course, but it was good to be back.

She carried the wine into the tiny living room. It was definitely good to be back amidst her own stuff—familiar, comfortable, and soothing. Only one box remained unpacked. She had deliberately left this box for the last. It contained all her the memorabilia from India. She opened it and took out the frame which carried her parents' photograph. Her parents smiled back at her from the picture, but the glass was cold against her fingers. She missed them. Even after so many years and going through so much. Would they have approved of her avenging them? Had she done the right thing?

The intense loathing she had felt for those men in Kashmir had consumed her for the past ten years. And now that the mission was over, she felt empty and lonely.

Nothing had gone according to plan. She felt like a puppet in the hands of life, performing to a drama whose plot she was not privy to.

She had thought revenge would give her much-needed respite from her nightmares and the grief of losing her parents, but the grief had not diminished and the nightmares had not disappeared; only the characters had changed. Instead of her parents she now saw Krishnan Uncle and Nikhil—both sometimes in mortal danger and sometimes dead. The only thing that brought cheer to her heart was that Nikhil was hale and hearty somewhere back home.

One day, when the dust settled, she would go back home. Meet all her relatives, her school friends and... Nikhil. She had recognized him immediately that day in the village. He had had his features changed a bit, but she had recognized him. She would have recognized those coffee-brown eyes anywhere.

Yes, she would meet him, even if he had settled down with someone by then and had a dozen children. Even then she would meet him and talk about transference and all the psychological terms they had discussed that day. He had said he had fallen in love with her, then had come with Karan like a stranger to rescue her. But then he had vanished again. Probably all his love had evaporated after he had helped her and returned the favor he must have felt he owed her. That must be the reason he had not come to meet her in so many months. Granted, her departure had been a bit hush-hush. But he knew the team and he could always have asked Uncle Krishnan.

Ungrateful man!

A tear trickled down her cheek. She had expected him to come after her. The day she had stepped into the car with Uncle Krishnan, she had hoped for a happily-ever-after with Nikhil. As the days went past, hope was slowly leaving her cold and bereft.

Her gaze fell on her parents' photograph again and loneliness expanded its hold over her heart. The past few months she had been busy gathering the threads of her new life—for the third time—but the long weekend had made her susceptible to weak emotions. She sat there weeping, wallowing in her grief and pitying her state of affairs. All her pent-up emotions gave way to more tears. After an hour of crying and cursing, she got up to take a bath and then eat the solitary dinner she had bought from the nearby Chinese joint.

A flicker on the laptop screen caught her attention.

Someone was at the front door, walking up the stairs. She wasn't expecting anyone. Her eyes went to the watch she wore. The tiny emergency button, disguised as the winding knob, was programmed to alert the nearest police station. Her hands went to her purse which had her gun.

As the man came into full view, she stood there frozen, with one hand clutching the purse and the other holding on to the counter to steady herself. He was someone familiar. Someone she had watched over and over in so many videos that she could recognize that gait anywhere. Her heart hammered against her rib-cage as she waited for him to ring the doorbell.

His scar was gone, and the face was a bit leaner, but those eyes were the same, making her heart do tap-dance since the day she had seen him without the blindfold. Now he sported a trimmed stubble too, very much in line with the current fashion. Clad in jeans and a black t-shirt, he looked so fit and virile, a far cry from the injured, limping man dressed in the brown *phiran*, she had watched that night crossing the road to the cantonment gate.

To her confusion, he stood there looking at the nameplate on the door. He then took a step back and raked his hair with his fingers. His demeanor alien to her. She had never seen him so unsure of himself. What was he doing standing there and doing nothing? She wanted him to ring the bell and come inside. She wanted him to show her that he had really fallen for her, and it had nothing to do with their ordeal in Kashmir. She wanted to ask him what took him so long to find her? She wanted—

Her thoughts ground to an abrupt halt as he turned around. Was he going?

He pivoted again facing the camera and rubbed his face as if tired beyond words. Then he turned and left the way he had come!

'*What the fuck!*' She released the death grip on the counter and rushed to unlock the door.

"Nikhil," she called out, her voice coming out in a hoarse whisper.

The door on the ground floor clicked shut and a car drove off. He was really gone!

She could have asked Krishnan uncle for his whereabouts, but what was the point. She wasn't sure about his feelings earlier. But now…

The phantom rock pressing against her chest became heavier.

***

CHAPTER EIGHTEEN

As Ziya entered her apartment after a long day at the university the next Friday, the loneliness which had receded to the back of her mind during the workday unfurled its tentacles once again. Seeing Nikhil had put her on high emotional alert. She had expected him to appear by her side every second for the past three days, but he hadn't obliged.

Eating solitary dinners and feeling sorry for herself would not help her cause, she thought in sudden rebellion. Why couldn't she go to the restro-bar down the lane and get to know the locals? The area was near her university, maybe she would bump into someone known to her from her first year.

Ziya scanned the restaurant but couldn't spot an unoccupied table. So intent was she on having a good time as she made her way toward the bar, that she failed to notice a pair of eyes watching her cross the dining hall. Her back toward the diners, she settled on one of the stools. She flicked through the menu but couldn't zero down on a drink to suit her mood.

"May I buy you a drink?" someone said.

She turned and stared. He looked just like she had pictured him—handsome in a navy-blue dinner jacket and light-blue shirt open at the neck.

He smiled. "Hi, I am Neal. Neal Mehra. May I join you?"

The bleakness of her life disappeared the very next moment. She wanted to launch herself into his arms. He, on the other hand, stood composed like a stranger who had a mild interest in this girl he had just seen. Sudden tears threatened to spill out from the corners of her eyes. She blinked and dropped her gaze to the mobile in her hands.

"Are you alright?" he asked softly.

She nodded and swallowed the salty liquid constricting her throat, then looked up again. "Actually, you reminded me of someone I had met a long time back," she said, going along with the charade.

"I hope they are good memories."

She nodded. "Yes, they are." She extended her hand. "Ziya Malik."

"I have a table here," he said, shaking her hand. "Would you care to join me?"

"Yeah. Sure." A tingle ran down her heart when he didn't loosen his grip on her hand.

He took her to a corner table and pulled a chair for her. The waiter followed them and handed him the menu. The ease with which he was handling the whole situation made her feel shy and gauche. The last date she remembered was with a boy from school when she was eighteen. After that, this was the first time she was dining at a fine restaurant, that too with a man who hobnobbed with Mumbai's elite.

On top of that, her conflicting emotions confused her. On one hand, she wanted to wrap herself around him and howl, on the other it felt she didn't know him at all, which definitely was a fact. Whatever she knew about him was gathered from the media, generic details that anyone would know.

"That's a long time to study a menu." His amused tone made her all the more flustered. "If I may…" He plucked the menu from her hand, rotated it, then handed it back to her.

"Oh…" She had been holding the menu upside down! Embarrassed to the core, she quickly tried to think of something to order and be done with it. "Er… I'll have a martini." She slapped the drinks menu down and picked up the other. Not only was she gauche, but stupid as well. He would lose all interest in her once he got to know her.

"How about wine? Will you prefer that?" he asked.

"Yeah, I don't mind."

"Red or white?"

"Any. You choose." There! Now she sounded sophisticated and confident.

"Ziya."

"What?" She raised her gaze to his face.

"You have beautiful eyes."

'Damn!' She dropped her gaze and pretended to study the menu again. Just when she was beginning to get her bearings, he had to go and says things like that. Thankfully the waiter came along to take their orders.

"So, are you studying or working?" he asked when the waiter left.

"Studying," she replied and looked around the hall.

"Which subject?"

"Computer Science."

She fell silent after that like the dumb girl she never thought she was.

"Now it's your turn to ask about me."

Her gaze jerked back to him. "About what?"

He smiled. "Anything! You can ask about my profession, my address, my family, or…" He lowered his voice and said softly, "Or maybe I can tell you what I like and—"

"So, what do you do?" she blurted, his sexy voice sending her into a tizzy.

"I'm into security, and have come here to explore my options," he answered studying her face, disconcerting her all the more.

"I wish you wouldn't look at me like that," she said.

"Like what?"

"As if you were searching for someone."

He chuckled, nodding his head. "You are so right. I am. One day I'll tell you the story."

She forgot the next question she had planned to ask, but luckily the waiter came to her rescue again, fetching their drinks. She sighed and picked up her glass as he raised his in a silent toast. Their eyes met over the glasses and her heart did a merry jig.

"So, do you agree to have dinner with strangers just like that?" he asked.

"Not with all," she said taking a sip, looking at anything but him.

"I'm honored. But the question remains, why did you agree to have dinner with me?"

Now she studied him openly, perhaps it was the wine which gave her the courage, and she smiled, "Are you fishing for compliments?"

"Maybe."

"Well, as I said you looked familiar."

"Don't you think it's dangerous courting strangers? For all you know I could be a murderer." He smiled.

She grinned. "And do *you* always have dinner with single females you spot in a bar? What if I turn out to be a serial killer?"

He chuckled. "I will happily die in your hands provided you agree to one of my conditions."

Ziya was drowning in the web of charm he was weaving around her. She toyed with her salad and asked, "What is it?"

"Spend the weekend with me."

She narrowed her eyes. "Do you think that'll be advisable? You being a stranger and all? Probably a killer."

"Then it's time to remedy that… lets' get to know each other… Ziya with the blue eyes," he added her name softly, causing her to blush.

"What about your girlfriend?" That topic had to be dealt with, else there would be no getting to know each other. Though Esha was out of the picture the day Ziya had seen Vikram and Esha's wedding pics on the Internet, there could be others.

"Girlfriend?" He frowned.

"You must be having one, I'm sure."

"There's no one. I've left everything behind in search of something new, someone unique."

The waiter cleared the table.

"Dessert?" he asked.

She shook her head, hardly noticing that she had finished most of the wine.

"Would you like to dance?"

Dance with him? She would never survive. They had so many things to discuss—so many unanswered questions between them. She shook her head.

"So, shall we leave?" he asked.

She nodded, unable to trust her voice.

They took a cab to her apartment,

Conscious of his eyes on her, Ziya sat far away from him, lest she lost control over her senses. The atmosphere was so electric that even the taxi driver sensed it and kept glancing at them in the rearview mirror.

"Would you like to come in for a nightcap?" she asked as she rummaged in her bag for the keys, dying to discuss everything that had happened back in the Valley and thereafter.

"Hmm… , okay," Nikhil answered against his wish. He didn't trust himself with her in the relative privacy of her apartment, but he didn't want to leave her either. He wanted nothing more than to be with her, but there were things to be sorted out, questions to be answered and lots of catching up to be done. Moreover, she was too young and inexperienced. She had gone to that mission at nineteen, barely out of the school.

"How about another glass of wine?" she asked placing her bag on the counter and habitually switching on the laptop.

"No." He moved into the living room keeping a healthy distance between them. "Your parents?" he asked picking up the photo frame.

"Yes," she whispered.

"I'm sorry, Ziya." He looked at her. Her pain reflected in the warmth of his eyes.

"Thank you."

"Are they the reason you took so many risks to save me?"

"I thought you wanted to get to know me."

"Yes, isn't this a good place to start?"

"Why talk about unpleasant memories?" She stepped forward.

He smiled, taking a step back. "Okay, you pick the topic."

She looked at him for a moment then shrugged. "Can't think of any."

"How about making plans for tomorrow? This is my first time in Canada, so I had picked up some of the brochures from the airport." He took out the pamphlets from the inner pocket of his jacket. It was the wrong suggestion. It only made her move to his side, her dark head bent over the flier in his hand, her perfume tantalizing him. He tried to concentrate. "How about St Jacob's farmer's market?"

"It's quite scenic. I had gone there on one of my school trips."

"So that's out. Let's pick something else."

"No, I would like to go there with you." She raised her eyes to him, mesmerizing him.

Involuntarily his hand went to her cheek. "When did you get rid of your nose pin?"

"The week I arrived here."

They stood looking at each other. The current of awareness swirling around.

"Tell me about that person you are searching for," she said, referring to the conversation they had had at the restaurant.

"I'm looking for the girl with a nose pin and long hair, who got me out of death's trap."

"I'm sure it was nothing as dramatic."

"Ask me," he whispered, then added, "I have pictured you so often in my head. You look so different, yet so special."

She closed her eyes as he caressed the soft skin on her cheek. His hand moved to her nape and pulled her forward. He rubbed her lips with his thumb, and she sucked in her breath. The fliers slipped from his fingers soundlessly to the floor.

Unable to control the direction the evening was taking he placed his lips on hers. She moved into him, catching hold of his lapels as if to support herself. His other hand snaked around her waist and pulled her to him. They both fell on the couch glued to each other, their hands all over each other.

At the back of his mind something nagged at him to slow down, to take control over this onslaught of passion. This was not how he had planned their first evening. Since she had not had a normal life these past few years, he had vowed he would go through the complete routine with her—dates, dinners, and dances—everything a young girl would want before they could slowly explore their feelings for each other.

Her hands were now tugging at his buttons and his were inside her top. He took deep breaths and tried to disentangle himself, but she stopped on her own accord.

"What's this?" She held the black thread on his neck and pulled it. The silver charm dangled on the string.

"Your first gift to me."

"Why are you still wearing it?" she asked, something dark replaced the passion in her eyes.

"It's a constant reminder that we have to be alert and cautious. Where's yours?"

"Somewhere in my closet. Do you think—"

A flicker of movement on her laptop caught his eyes, halting their conversation.

"What's that?!" he said, frowning.

"What?" She looked up from the charm at him.

"You have a live camera feed on your laptop."

"Yes. So?" She straightened back on the couch pulling her top down.

"Do you have a backup too?"

She looked at him then put her tongue in her cheek. "I saw you the other day."

He looked at her for a moment, then grinned sheepishly. "No wonder you weren't that surprised to see me tonight. You recognized me so easily."

"Of course. Some things never change… if one knows a person."

The way she looked into his eyes, he understood what she was trying to say.

"Why did you run away?" she asked.

"Coming inside the apartment on the first day of our meeting was the wrong move. After three months of looking for you, I wasn't thinking straight." He ran his fingers through his hair and sighed. "Hell, I'm not thinking straight even now. I want to do the right things by you."

"What right things?" she frowned.

"We should be meeting casually first, getting to know each other like normal people."

"Why? Is that a written rule? We have not had a normal life. At least I haven't." She pulled him to her and ran a finger on his chest. "And normal is boring."

He caught hold of her hand sneaking inside his shirt again. "We barely know each other, Ziya. Hell, I still refer to you as Ayesha in my mind then correct myself before speaking."

A sliver of pain slashed through her eyes, but she masked it in the next moment and bent down to pick up the pamphlets. "Do you also see me as Rehaan Muhammad's widow rather than ACP Malik's daughter?"

"What a ridiculous question! Of course you are ACP Malik's daughter. And I see no connection of that terrorist with you. You should forget those years there like a bad dream."

"Shouldn't you do the same thing?" She raised her eyelashes suddenly looking like an imp, who had scored a point.

"Yes, for that we have to make fresh memories. Fresh and normal. And also…"

"Also?"

"Do you know how old I am?"

"Yes. You are thirty years and two months old."

"How do you know that?"

"My major at the University is computer hacking. So what about your age?"

"The thing is…" he trailed off.

Her frown deepened into a scowl.

"Don't you think I'm too old for you?"

She began to laugh. "Yes. You are an old uncle," she replied, gasping for breath.

"It's not something to laugh at." He scowled. "We'll go out with each other like normal people do and if we like each other then this will go forward."

"Okay." She sat back. "Let's get to know each other, Neal Mehra."

"You mean now?"

"Yes. No better time than today." She twitched her shoulders and smoothened her skirt.

"No, no… today is not a good time. I'm tired and it's quite late."

"Okay." She smiled then whispered, "Uncle."

He ignored and struggled not to give in his un-uncle like feelings. He never thought they would discuss the matter so plainly, and that she would agree so readily. "Okay then, I'll take your leave." He held her hand and planted a kiss on the back. "I'll pick you up at ten tomorrow morning," he said and left.

Bemused, Ziya stood there pondering over his logic and the fact that he was so earnest about it. No matter how hard he denied, they had a history of about seven-months between them. She didn't feel the need of knowing him like… like normally.

Was he really serious about this dating crap? Wasn't he dying to take her into his arms as she wanted him?

***

CHAPTER NINETEEN

Since it was a day trip, Ziya decided on a white sundress with rose patterns all over and strappy sandals that crisscrossed up till her calf, enjoying the loose attire after being confined to heavy phirans and dupattas for so many years.

Perhaps he wanted to date her and get to know her, but she had other plans. She was sure about her feelings and knew him well enough. She didn't have the patience for a long-drawn-out courtship. The sexy sundress was appropriate for both their plans.

He rang her doorbell exactly at ten in the morning. She saw him in the camera feed on her laptop. He looked divine in a white t-shirt and blue jeans. She sighed happily and ran to the door.

"Hi." Her voice was hoarse. She tried to clear her throat unobtrusively.

"Hey." He handed her the lilies he had brought, then stood looking at her, studying her features one by one, the same way he had done the previous night. Was it last night?

"Would you like to have some coffee before we push off?" she asked.

"No, I'm good."

She smiled hiding her disappointment. "Okay then, I'll put these flowers in water then we can go." He didn't even follow her inside.

At the St Jacob's farmer's market, they went on a buggy ride on the traditional Mennonite carriage. She had been to this place earlier, but today the outing had a different flavor altogether. She sat enjoying his presence as he pointed out various attractions and the scenic landscape.

The moment she would come in contact with his arm or his t-shirt, or inhale a whiff of his perfume, she wanted to wrap herself around him. The problem was not proximity, but lack of privacy. So later in the coach she sat a little too close for his comfort—she could make out from the looks he sent her way—but he didn't move away.

They drove through farms and on quiet country roads, listening to the sound of the horse's hooves. And they talked.

He asked her about her childhood, steering clear of the period from her parents' death till her rescue. She, in turn, asked about his parents. They visited a sugar bush and ate pancakes and maple syrup. The whole day was sinfully beautiful and painfully erotic for her.

He, on the other hand, didn't seem to have any problem whatsoever. He made love to her the whole day with his eyes, with a touch here and a caress there, and later he left her home with a peck on her lips and a promise to pick her up at seven-thirty for dinner.

What was wrong with him? Weren't guys supposed to be higher on hormones compared to girls? Her emotionally charged brain was getting fried with his blow hot, blow cold behavior. From now onwards, she vowed, she would be the one in control of the proceedings.

***

After taking a leisurely bath with scented bath salts, she took out the black Chantilly lace dress she had saved for special occasions. The slip was a strapless thigh-length affair, showing off her modest cleavage. The full sleeved A-line lace dress came to her knees, covering her, yet showing glimpses of her curves. Silver loopy earrings and stilettos completed her ensemble. Her hair, now touching her shoulders, fell in simple s-curves all around her face. A little mascara and pink lip-gloss were enough to give the subtle, yet tantalizing, look she wanted.

Nikhil's in-drawn breath as she opened her front door that evening boosted her confidence. This time she locked the door without extending the invitation to come inside for a pre-dinner drink.

He took her to a happening restaurant which boasted of a dance floor and live music.

"Do you think we should talk about things which we have been avoiding for the past twenty-four hours?" she began the moment they sat down and ordered the drinks and starters. She wanted to do away with any serious stuff he had in mind and enjoy the night later. As far as she was concerned, she had canned the last ten years of her life and forgotten about it.

"I don't think that's a good idea."

"Do you suspe—"

"It's a public place and I have booked the table in advance," he interrupted.

"We could have discussed it during our ride in the morning." She couldn't help but pout, sulking a little.

"Ziya please, let's wait till tomorrow. It's a Sunday, we'll have all the time in the world."

She nodded, as the waiter came with their drinks and hors d'oeuvres.

"What?" she asked as he sat looking at her with amused indulgence.

"There is something different about you tonight."

She gulped down the drink in her mouth rather painfully. "Is it?"

"It reminds me of a night back in India when I was on a boat. The person with me was quite a force to reckon with."

"So, what did you do?" she smiled.

"It is better to just follow the lead when a woman gets bossy."

"How was the experience?"

He smiled and said after a pause, "Quite sexy."

This time she held his gaze with an answering one of her own. The evening went from flirtatious to downright hot. They discussed their favorite movies and books through the meal when all they really wanted was to hold each other tight.

Half an hour later, the music pulled them onto the dance floor, but it was torture to be so close to each other, yet unable to do something about it.

"Do you want to leave?" he whispered against her ear, as his hands increased their pressure on her waist.

She nodded.

It was an ordeal to keep their hands off each other during the short ride home. It was an equally arduous task to find the key to her door. But, as she turned around with the key, he said. "So, when do I pick you up tomorrow?"

"Where are you going?" she asked.

"I think we should call it a night."

"Don't you think it's time we didn't?" She scowled.

"Talking happens tomorrow. We agreed."

"I'm not interested in that 'talking'." She caught hold of his lapel. "We'll have a different kind of talk tonight." She clicked the door open.

"I… I don't think that's a good idea."

"Why not?"

"You are courting with danger."

"I have done that for most of my life. I'm a veteran."

"Still, I don't think we should rush this."

In answer, she caught hold of his jacket, pulled him inside and shut the door. Nikhil stood just inside the door afraid to do something which might annoy her. She stared at him for a moment then tossed her purse on the couch. Her wrap followed the purse.

Taking a step forward, she slid her hand under his jacket, around his neck and pulled him flush against her length. "You know you did this to me in one of my dreams." Her breath fanned his neck. His palms fisted.

"Really?" He couldn't recognize his voice and cleared his throat.

It was then she realized how much he wanted her. And how tightly he had kept his passion in check with sheer willpower. It was time to unleash everything.

"And then you did something like this." She went on her toes and gently rubbed her lips on his.

"Then what happened?" he asked breathlessly against her lips.

"Then I hugged you and opened my mouth." She was smiling.

He couldn't help but do the same.

Then there was no stopping.

She took off his jacket. He pulled down her zip and pushed her against the wall kissing her cheek, neck, pushing off her dress down her shoulders. In answer, she unbuttoned his shirt and caressed his chest.

He picked her up and moved toward the bedroom when his legs refused to support them. They fell on the bed in unison, exploring each other. Cursing, she tugged at his shirt when she couldn't undo the last two buttons; her dress down till her elbows didn't allow her full access. As she struggled with the clothes, he surfaced from the magic of the moment.

"Don't you think we should take it a bit slow?" He held her hand roaming on his abs.

"Why?"

"You are too young."

"I'm going to be twenty-three in four months' time!"

He sighed but didn't say anything.

"Don't you like me?"

"Not like you? Sunshine, I've come all this way just to be with you, but your lack of experience is terrifying me!"

She jerked back, pursed her lips and stared at him.

"I mean… er… I know," he stuttered.

"What do you know?" she narrowed her eyes.

"I know that you left school at eighteen and you have been there almost all your adult life. I know that… you are a… er…"

"I'm what?"

"Inexperienced," he finished lamely.

"You want me to get rid of my virginity and then meet you again?"

"Hell." He raked his fingers through his hair. "Do you have to put it in quite that way?"

"Why? Have you never come across a virgin in India?" she said, tongue-in-cheek. It was fun to see him squirm in embarrassment for a change.

"Gosh, Ziya! Do we have to discuss this right now when we are half naked?"

All of a sudden, she smiled, took off her dress and launched herself at him again, squishing the air out of his lungs. "I had imagined this night since the time I saw your photographs on the internet."

"Did you? I'm floating amongst nine clouds."

She giggled, then quietened down as he kissed her with a thoroughness that made her aware how inexperienced she really was. But she was a quick learner and repeated whatever he did to her, on him.

"Ah Ziya, you are killing me." He took a deep breath and caught hold of her face away from his, putting some distance between them. Caressing a lock of hair falling on her forehead. "It's a pity you had to cut your hair. I had dreamt of running my fingers through it so many times."

What now? He was using delaying tactics again when she was almost naked and they were in the bedroom. Still. "Really? What else did you dream of?"

"I imagined it spread over my chest or on the pillow, the whole long, soft, silky length."

"What else?"

"Your eyes—" He broke off when she rolled the said organ. "What—"

"Keep quiet." She got up and undid the rest of the buttons of his shirt. "Just keep quiet and touch me. And don't worry about the rest of the stuff, I'm on pills."

Nikhil groaned and did as she bid him to. He loved this bossy girl.

***

Something woke him up. The heavy drapes on the windows didn't allow him to guess whether the dawn was about to break or was it still middle of the night. Ziya slept on the other side pulling the comforter along with her. He looked at her as she stirred and groaned again. It was her voice which had woken him up.

"Ziya?" To his alarm, she suddenly reached out for something and said, 'no'. She was dreaming. Not a pleasant dream. She had gone through stressful years back in the valley, unable to be herself, wearing that mask of an uneducated village belle always on high alert.

"Ziya, it's okay." He gathered her in his arms, she calmed down muttering some gibberish.

He caressed her as she slept like a doll. Curled up on one side, looking small and vulnerable. He looked at his wristwatch. It was 6:15 a.m. They had fallen asleep in the wee hours of the morning, he could have slept some more but not today. He just wanted to watch the woman in his arms—his woman.

So habitual had he been to think of her as Ayesha that he still had trouble in reconciling to her urbane avatar. He brushed back her short hair covering her cheek and eyes. The most shocking was the absence of the nose-ring. It suited her a lot but he had to live with it. Her safety was of utmost priority. He couldn't resist the surge of affection and rubbed his thumb on her lips. She stirred and opened her eyes.

"Hey, sorry I disturbed you. Go back to sleep."

"Whas d time?" she slurred, closing her eyes again.

"It's a little after six a.m."

"Nikhil? Oh, I should remember to call you Neal. Neal?"

"Hmm…"

"I think you don't have emotional transference for me."

"Are we having that talk?"

"Its Sunday, isn't it?"

He chuckled. "So it is."

She propped herself up on her elbow and looked at him silently.

He raised his eyebrows when she continued to watch him.

"You were right. Your captivity reminded me of my father's ordeal. He died because of the torture. I couldn't let that happen to you. But I think I fell in love with you a little every day."

He rolled over kissing her, and spoke against her lips, "You were like a goddess, Sunshine. I can't be thankful enough for the day you came into my life."

"But it's not transference that you feel for me. Or it wouldn't have lasted this long."

"Yes, you are right. I adore you, Ziya Malik. And it'll last forever."

Satisfied with the logic, she sighed and lay her head on his chest.

"What took you so long to come here?"

"It took me some time to find your address."

"You could have asked Uncle Krishnan."

He frowned at the name. It took him about three seconds to connect the name with Rao. K.N. Rao, of course, was her precious Uncle Krishnan. The old coot.

She felt him stiffened. "Ni—"

"Don't take his name in front of me. I can't stand him."

Her head jerked up and scowled. "That won't do. He is like a father to me."

"Okay, calm down." She looked so worried that he had to pretend everything was fine. "It's okay."

"But why?"

"Just forget about it. It's just an old grudge."

'Old grudge'. The phrase opened the can of memories she had sealed last night. She fell silent contemplating her days spent in the Valley. The terror of the initial days, when she had been worried every minute of saying or doing something wrong and being found out. And then, all those days under the shadow of Rehaan's attention.

Nikhil sensed her mood and hugged her tight. "Problem?"

She shook her head.

"Want to talk about it?"

"No… it's nothing."

He turned her over and kissed her neck.

She giggled.

"Ticklish, are we?" He nuzzled some more, and they rolled over the bed kissing and laughing.

A few moments later the laughter subsided as their senses soared to a different plane.

***

CHAPTER TWENTY

"Uncle Krishnan!" she shrieked and launched herself at him.

"Steady, *beta*. I'm not that young now."

"What a pleasant surprise! Come in, come in. It's raining!" She took his coat and brushed off the water droplets, as Rao stepped inside and closed the door. "How is Delhi?"

"Hot and humid. Have you settled well?"

"Yes, of course." She flashed a glance at the bedroom door.

He took her chin in his hand and tilted her face toward the light to look at her nose piercing. "Dr. Maurya has done a good job. It's not visible at all."

"Yes, he has. No, it's not visible."

He stood admiring her transformation. She had chopped her hair short and looked every inch a woman born and brought up in the western world, a far cry from the Kashmiri village belle.

"Though the risk is negligible, remember every precaution that I have taught you, every day without fail."

"Yes, of course." She wrung her hands. "What would you like to have? I have your favorite Belgian coffee." She looked again toward the bedroom as she moved toward the kitchen.

"Ask him to come out."

"Who?" She swung around.

"The man in your bedroom."

"Oh." She filled the kettle, avoiding his eyes. "He's still sleeping."

Rao stood at the window scanning the orange-yellow and green expanse spread before him. Beautiful in the autumn morning. It had begun to rain again. "How is your course?"

"Perfect. The workload is not much at the moment." As she handed him the mug of coffee, she heard the room open.

"Ziya, is the tap giving you hell again?" Nikhil entered pulling a t-shirt over his naked torso, making her go red.

"No," she spat, remembering in the nick of a second to answer him.

"Oh, the boss has come to take an update," Nikhil smirked as he spotted Rao in the living room.

"Neal!" She softly reprimanded him but was surprised that Uncle Krishnan wasn't perturbed at all by Nikhil's presence.

"Never mind, Ziya. Hi Neal, how are you?"

"Better than I have ever been. Not that I particularly like the current situation. At least I can be myself with you. I hate pretensions."

"Agreed, you can be howsoever you please with me," Rao said. "Relax Ziya, and if you have some to spare, give him a mug of coffee too. Maybe he will sound less like a boor after having one."

"Don't bother, Ziya. You sit here." Nikhil jerked his head toward the general direction of the sofa. "I can't stand him. I can feed myself in the kitchen."

"Neal?"

Worried, she watched him disappear into the kitchen. How would she live if the two men she loved didn't get along with each other?

"Relax, he'll be fine. Come here." Rao patted the sofa beside him.

Ziya settled in the crook of his arm with her head on his chest, as she had done when her parents had died. "How are you, my princess? You have done well. You have done what no one could have done, ever. Hussein would have been so proud." He caressed her hair and kissed her temple.

"Why is Neal acting that way toward you?" She scowled, ignoring the praise he lavished on her. In any case, she didn't want to talk about her parents.

"He is blaming me for putting you in harm's way."

She sat up. "Really?!"

Rao nodded. "And I didn't give him your address after that day."

She laughed out loud, hugging him hard. "You are so mean."

He chuckled. "That I am. What he doesn't know is that it was I who scattered the crumbs so that he could trace you."

"You really are one mean goat, but an adorable one." She hugged him again. "But why?"

"There were many reasons. One, I wanted to see if our system was foolproof if someone tried to trace you, which it is because he couldn't locate you, not without my covert help. The second reason was that I wanted to test his resolve to find you, to gauge the strength of his feelings for you. And the last and most important reason was that I was worried that in his eagerness to meet you, he might blow your cover. I wanted you to get to Canada and safety first. I wanted you to settle down a little..." He paused and looked at her tenderly. "The truth is, Ziya, I wanted you to have some time to yourself... to sort out your feelings."

She dropped her gaze to her hands.

"I wanted to be sure you were taking the right decision for the right reasons. After all, you are so young, and you have gone through so much... Ziya, you have to talk about those years. Let it get out of your system. Unfortunately, I can't even ask you to go to a counselor. Talk to him." He tilted his head toward the kitchen. "He is a good listener."

She nodded and switched the topic to her job and daily routine. Rao let her steer the conversation to lighter things, satisfied that he had sowed the seeds for her bright and happy future.

"Ziya!" Nikhil called from the kitchen.

"Go, he's getting jealous," Rao said.

"Hah! Jealous of an old goat? Never!" Nikhil shouted again.

"Neal!" Amused, Ziya ran to the kitchen. "Why are you behaving like this?"

Ignoring the issue, Nikhil caught hold of her and planted a silent kiss on her lips.

"We shouldn't," she whispered, but couldn't stop at one and clung to him till they had to come up for air.

"I can't find turmeric," he said getting his breath back.

She turned toward the cupboards. "What are you making?"

"Biryani."

"Could you please be pleasant to him?"

He raised his brows.

"It was as much my decision to go on the mission as his." She pleaded. "I was nineteen, an adult. Please, for my sake."

He kissed her nose. "Anything for you, sweetheart."

The emotions thawed over hot biryani and ice-wine—an eclectic combination. Nikhil participated in the conversation, though he kept his distance from Rao.

K. N. Rao smiled as he left the apartment and sat in the car. He couldn't have hoped for a better bodyguard for his darling.

***

Request For Feedback/ Review

Thank you for taking the time to read 'Guardian Angel'. Word of mouth is an author's best friend and much appreciated. If you enjoyed it, please consider telling your friends and/or posting a short review on Amazon or Goodreads.

Thank you,

Ruchi Singh.

www.ruchisingh.com

GLOSSARY

Ammi	:	Mother
Angithi	:	Earthen, portable oven used for cooking
Beta	:	Son, or daughter
Bhai	:	Brother
Burqah	:	Outer garment worn by Muslim women which covers them from head to toe
Chacha	:	Paternal Uncle
Dua	:	Prayer
Dupatta	:	Stole, long scarf
Hukkah	:	a long stemmed instrument for vaporizing and smoking flavored tobacco
Jaan	:	Sweetheart
Kangri	:	An earthen pot woven around with wicker filled with hot embers used by Kashmiris beneath their traditional clothing to keep the chill at bay
Kazi	:	Priest
Khala	:	Aunt, mother's sister
Khakhi	:	light sandy brown color, primarily used for army and police uniforms
Nikah	:	Wedding
Phiran	:	Warm outer garment worn by people in Kashmir
Saab	:	Sir
Salaam	:	Greeting
Sharara	:	A Muslim traditional dress

Sherwani	:	Long coat, normally worn at festive occasions
Shikara	:	Boat
Taveez	:	Charm, normally worn to ward off bad-luck

ACKNOWLEDGEMENTS

There is a sense of unmatched accomplishment as I sit to write the last piece for this novel. This is the first time I have had the full-fledged character in a known situation and then I had to create the plot-line, usually it is the other way round.

So the first vote of thanks goes to my readers who were not pleased the way Nikhil's role panned out in Book 1 of Undercover series, 'The Bodyguard' and motivated me to write this story. I'm forever indebted for their insistence and inspiration.

I would like to thank my beta readers Shantala Nayak, Deep Downer, Devika Fernando and Tulika Singh for their insightful feedback. My special thanks goes to my editor Vrinda Baliga for putting my project on priority, and for her honest critique and flawless editing.

Last but not the least I am indebted to my family and core group of writers for your support—you all know who you are, and I don't need to state your names, love you all.

Books By Ruchi Singh

English

Novels

Romantic Suspense

The Bodyguard - Undercover Series # 1

Guardian Angel - Undercover Series # 2

Romance

Jugnu - The Firefly

Take 2 - Small Town Girl #1

My Love, A Liar - Small Town Girl #2

Bewitched

Short Stories

Women From Mars : Series Shorts

Temptation

Spark

Hearts & Hots - Series Shorts

Head Over Heels

You and Only You

Silent Love

A Promise is a Promise

हिंदी

एहसास - मेहरा ख़ानदान # १

काली नज़र - मेहरा ख़ानदान # २

लफ़ंगा - मेहरा ख़ानदान # ३

टेक २ - नज़रों का खेल (जल्द ही ऐमज़ॉन पर)

Bonus Chapter from 'The Bodyguard' by Ruchi Singh

October 1st

Golf Club, New Delhi

1st October, 12:25 PM

He had been *following Vikramaditya Seth Jr. for years, watching, waiting. Patiently. Tenaciously. Not a tough task since it was a conscious decision.*

He knew everything about Seth Jr.—the residences, offices, cars, relatives, friends. The only hitch in his plan was Seth's routine, which was as unpredictable as the national stock exchange index.

Seth Jr. liked to be in his office early in the morning, but the timing was never the same. The choice of conveyance, by land or air, always varied with no fixed pattern. The guards sanitized the meeting venues and locations, like he was the POTUS. Even the dates with the numerous lady-friends were unplanned. It never failed to amaze one at the way women readily fell in line with his erratic schedule.

The blame, or credit, for the unpredictability lay on that devious Nikhil Mahajan, Seth's security-in-charge, his right-hand-man and a smart, arrogant sonofabitch.

He smirked. He liked sonofabitches. They gave him the opportunity to outsmart them. And today he was confident he would beat Mahajan, for he had changed his strategy. Instead of focusing on Seth, he had begun to concentrate on the people around Seth. Predictable beings. Predictable, boring beings like Sunil Baggah, a businessman, who was meeting Seth today.

Baggah always had Sunday lunch at Delhi Golf Club's open-air restaurant, at one p.m., at table number seven. Today Baggah had invited Seth there.

He looked at his wristwatch. A few more minutes of waiting left.

Taking his eyes off the viewfinder, he studied his surroundings. The green belt next to the golf course, maintained by the horticulture department, was like a mini-forest, devoid of all life except for the usual chirping birds and scurrying squirrels. Lush mint-green trees bathed from last night's downpour swayed in rhythm to the gentle breeze. The afternoon sunshine sieved through the canopy of thick leaves, casting a warm glow inside the thicket.

The wide branches of the Banyan tree he was perched on gave him adequate cover from anyone paying attention from the golf course. He had had the place under surveillance for the past one month and was confident of no human interruptions or surprises. Yesterday's rain had given him a sleepless night, but today the skies were as clear as it could get. He took it as a divine blessing from Maa.

An imperceptible movement brought his gaze to the nearby branch. A chameleon sat like a carved statue merging with the ebony brown of the bark. Excited at the chance of a little sport, he reached slowly towards his feet and took out the knife from the case strapped to his boot. Without taking his eyes off the creature, he struck out in one clean sweep.

Khatchak!

Wriggling, the upper half of the chameleon fell to the ground. Blood poured out from the remaining half still glued to the branch, stunned into a stupor. The red liquid oozing out of an animal always surprised him. Shouldn't the color be different from us humans? He nudged the half-carcass down with the knife's tip and wiped the blade on the bark before sheathing it inside its leather cover.

Rejuvenated, he inhaled the fresh air. The faint misty mud-fragrance rising from the wet ground reminded him of a distant childhood memory when he had lifted a stone in the park where he played and seen earthworms crawling underneath. He had enjoyed smashing each one of them with the stone. They didn't have red blood in them, he remembered and sighed. Fingering the rudraksh string around his neck, he blanked his mind and focused on the task ahead.

He had a clear view of the white wicker tables set inside the boundary of the golf course, just shy of a thousand yards from his location. Once the men were seated at the table, the multi-colored garden umbrellas would cease to matter for an uninterrupted sight. Though the direction of the wind was perfect, he was concerned about the speed. But then it would be no fun if there was no challenge.

Mentally revising the exit route one more time, he looked back and located his car beyond the woods—a nondescript white Tata Indica, which he would ditch at a pre-planned location and hire a public transport.

Assured, he looked around again. Not a single soul stirred in the region. Have the squirrels gone for their siesta or have they sensed his intent? Even the chirping birds had gone quiet in-sync with their cohabitants. Was it time for action? He glanced towards the cluster of tables, his karmabhoomi, and frowned.

Two golf carts stood on the paved pathway near the tables. Were they early? Maybe a few minutes. It didn't bother him. He checked the flash-sound-suppressor of his .338 Magnum, aligned the scope, aimed the cross-hair at table number seven, and positioned his trigger-finger.

It was time to end the long wait.

Maa Kaali had waited long enough for the bali. And a fitting sacrifice she would get.

'Om Krim Kaaliaaye Namah!'

Golf Club Entrance

1st October, 12:45pm

"Madam, change," the auto-rickshaw driver shouted, handing out a five-rupee coin.

"Keep it," Esha said, jumping out of the vehicle.

Anxious about the outcome of her interview, she absentmindedly signed the visitors' register at Delhi Golf Club's entrance gate. The guard directed her towards the open-air restaurant, where she was meeting someone for a job opening. Her savings were dwindling fast, and she was desperate.

Walking on the paved path, as she did a last-minute check on her resume and certificates in the file, she rammed into someone. "Goddamn!" The file and papers flew out of her hand as she lost her footing and tumbled backward.

"Steady..." Hard, confident hands held her shoulders as she tried fielding the scattering papers, pen, and file.

Flustered, she looked up at the familiar yet elusive face. Hooded eyes, partially visible behind the steel-grey shades perched on a sharp nose, looked straight into hers. Something traversed down to her toes, something strong, something powerful. An acute self-awareness overcame her and the apology died on her lips.

The only response she got for her tongue-tied stare was a knowing, slight upward movement of one corner of his mouth. Contrary to her nature, the pounding heartbeat for a complete stranger baffled her. But before the recognition dawned that she had crashed into the legendary industrialist Vikramaditya Seth Jr., his security retinue swept her aside gently and ushered him towards the open-air restaurant.

Watching him walk away, she recalled how the media had gone gaga over him when he had taken command of Seth Industries after his father's death earlier this year. A prodigy, with an exceptionally high IQ and command over no less than four languages, he was professed to be a brilliant strategist with a farsighted vision. Yesterday, she recalled watching a small clip of news showing his presence in Delhi in relation to a mega-infrastructure project in Myanmar.

Her heart thudded again when, without breaking his stride, he turned and glanced at her. She wasn't sure if she felt hot because of her blazer or him.

Not willing to give him an upper hand——for the second time—she held the eye contact, lifted her chin and schooled her face to present the blank, poker expression she was famous for until he and his entourage moved out of her sight.

***

Vikramaditya Seth didn't have the patience for whining complainers, even if one was an intelligent, whining complainer. Throughout their pathetic game of golf, which Sunil Baggah didn't know how to play, he had gabbed on and on about fictitious people threatening him because of the contract they were to sign soon. Even Nikhil, following them, had begun rolling his eyes and coughing suggestively. Scared to the core, Baggah told them that he had filed an FIR asking for additional police protection.

"If you want to back out, now is the time, Sunil. I won't mind," Vikram said, standing at the restaurant table reserved in Baggah's name.

"No... no... Vikram. You know I'm no coward." Baggah pulled a chair.

'No, you are a greedy coward.' Vikram sighed and gestured to Nikhil to take a seat at the table, but as always Nikhil refused and positioned himself right behind Vikram's chair, scanning the surroundings.

"Mahajan, you should relax... have a salad or a drink." Baggah opened the menu card.

Nikhil refused again. The guy was so obsessed with Vikram's security that it sometimes got onto Vikram's nerves too.

Baggah continued. "No one will have the courage to take on the mighty Vikram Seth in broad daylight. It is us—mere mortals—people down below the chain who have to be..."

Tuning-off Baggah's monotonous nattering, Vikram studied the white picket fenced restaurant and the gardens. The area was huge, a typical characteristic of Delhi clubs. The green lawns looked beautiful under the balmy sun. He sighed again. How he wished he could enjoy the spectacular day without the ever-nagging business discussions, and partners like Baggah eating up his time! Just him, a glass of rum... alone or perhaps with a partner who would understand and want him the way he was—moody, short-tempered, overbearing. Adjectives attributed to him by his mother and ex-wife—not that he agreed with them.

When was the last time he had taken a vacation? He couldn't recall.

"So what would you like to have?"

Baggah's raspy drawl brought him back to the question of lunch. He glanced at the menu and grimaced at the same old continental cuisine. A sudden memory of yellow *tadka daal* with *ghee*-laden *rotis* and his father scolding him for not eating veggies caught him unawares. He wondered at his unusually emotional chain of thoughts. He really needed a break.

The crackle of a sizzler dish and the aroma of roasted onions, from the adjacent table, made him glance at the menu. He placed his order for the first course.

It must have rained last night, Vikram thought as he went back to admiring the surroundings. The green landscaped gardens appeared fresh and nude like... like the face of the girl who had bumped into him. It wasn't surprising that she tip-toed into his thoughts so smoothly. She was distinctive. With her dusky, clear skin devoid of any trace of makeup, and short hair curling around her face, she looked nothing like the women in his coterie of acquaintances. And those honey-brown, deep eyes. A sliver of primitive desire ran through his toes.

Her flabbergasted, tongue-tied response was nothing new. People reacted to him that way many a time. But even during those astonished, dumb moments, she exuded confidence and elegance from every aspect of her demeanor. He couldn't fathom what made him glance at her again earlier. She had recovered her composure and had met his glance squarely and confidently. Admirable. He wouldn't mind her with him on his dream holiday. And, of course, the glass of rum on the rocks.

He did a double take when the woman occupying his mind entered the restaurant area and scanned the tables. He frowned. Was she looking for him? Looking to further their two-second acquaintance? His lips contorted in distaste. Perhaps the collision wasn't as innocent as he had been made to believe. But her reaction looked too natural and genuine to be pre-meditated. Maybe she was an actress.

No one could blame him for mistrusting women. The fairer-sex had fallen for him left-right-center throughout his life, even when he was married.

Bringing his gaze to the menu card in his hand, he waited for her to seek him out, gasp and approach him with feigned familiarity. He scowled when, after a few seconds, he heard no breathless greeting. He glanced up to find her marching to a table to his left, lean and lithe clad in a navy blue blazer and grey trousers, completely oblivious of his presence. A middle-aged bald man stood up at the table she was headed towards.

As she walked behind Vikram's chair something hit his elbow knocking the menu card off his hand, and something heavy dropped down on his left with a thump.

"Ah..."

Hearing the muffled groan, Vikram turned to see her sprawled on the ground. He bent down to help her. Baggah stood up shouting.

Then all hell broke loose!

Everything happened at once. One moment, Baggah was yelling. The next moment, he went quiet and fell face-down on the table. Someone gasped. His hand, outstretched to help the woman, shook and his heart slammed against the ribcage. Nikhil shouted. Vikram heard a faint whistle. His chair jerked. White cotton stuffing flew all over. The back cushion of Vikram's chair had been ripped apart.

Screaming and bellowing instructions to the guards, Nikhil pushed Vikram down. His head rammed into the fallen girl's stomach. She gasped and grunted again. After a second of stunned silence, she wriggled out from under his weight and moved towards Baggah. The pristine white tablecloth had turned red under Baggah's chest.

As the waiters and the club guards converged towards their table, Nikhil pulled Vikram up and steered him out of the restaurant. Vikram glanced back and saw the girl, in the blue blazer, sprinting like a gazelle towards the massive green Banyan grove near the barbed wire fence of the Golf Club.

***

Police Station, New Delhi

1st October, 6:00pm

"Ms. Sinha, what were you doing at the club?" The pot-bellied sub-inspector thumped the scarred, rickety wooden table with his fist, after his boss, the senior inspector, had left.

The young officer standing beside Esha cringed at the sudden noise. A recruit, she guessed. The lady constable standing in one corner, least bothered about the discussion or the situation, nibbled on the nails of her right hand.

Good thinking by them that they had stationed the woman or Esha would have added one more charge to her list of complaints that she was determined to file against the police after her release.

The sub-inspector repeated the question. Sitting straight on the hard iron chair, she ignored the pain in her hip and unflinchingly met the sub-inspector's gaze. His nostrils flared and trembled all the more at her blank stare.

The guards at the Golf Club had detained her after the violent incident and had confiscated her mobile phone. Later, the police had brought her to the station and had been interrogating her for the past three hours. They didn't allow her to contact anyone. She wasn't worried though, her family was only interested in the pay-check she brought.

Ignoring the sub-inspector glaring at her, she looked around the dingy, dusty cell in the police station. The bulb hanging from the high ceiling threw pale golden shadows all over, not doing anything for the dismal ambience of the room. The offensive stench drifting from the small round ventilator, high up on the back wall, indicated that the urinals were next to the lock-up—a deliberate ploy to weaken the fainthearted. But what they refused to believe was that she was not some common criminal or an ordinary female.

"Ma'am please, tell us the truth. It is in your interest." The young officer stepped towards her, playing the part of good cop to perfection.

"I've already told you everything," she answered, just to ease his distress.

The senior inspector had asked the same question several times before someone called him away. The bruise on her cheek throbbed, along with the anger she felt at the fools. Besides the knock on her hip, her midriff ached when she took deep breaths. Her ribs had probably taken a blow when the man fell on her. On top of all this, she had eaten nothing after breakfast. Her stomach grumbled in agreement.

For once, she cursed her habit of taking charge of a situation that was not her responsibility. But years of training had kicked in the moment she saw blood when the other man had keeled over. Trying to estimate the direction of the bullet and running towards the woods was a wrong move. They believed her to be an accomplice, whereas she had acted on impulse the moment she had realized the direction from where the shots were fired and had gone after the culprit. She had scanned the woods but hadn't seen anything or anyone. Some unknown force had stopped her before she could climb the fence, or it would have been really incriminating for her.

"Who sent you there?"

Esha stared at her hands. They hadn't put handcuffs on her wrists.

The lady constable fidgeted, shifting her weight on her left foot and began the mouth-manicure of the other hand. At this rate, she wouldn't be left with any nails, Esha thought, but couldn't blame her for the boredom. The woman had not budged from her position since the time Esha had been brought into the police lock-up.

"Whom are you working with? Why did you run towards the woods? Who was there?" With each question, the sub-inspector stabbed the scarred wooden desk with his flimsy pen. The tip broke at the final question.

Esha glanced at him, taking in the scowling gaze, fisted hands and sweating arm-pits. His condescending attitude was getting on her nerves.

"Am I under arrest? Do you have a warrant? If yes, I need a lawyer and if not, then you cannot detain me."

"So you will teach me the law? Will you... you bitch?" The fatso sneered. "Why were you there? Whom are you working for?"

"Ma'am please..." The other officer appeared genuinely embarrassed at the insult the fat sub-inspector had hurled at her.

She exhaled, knowing that rubbing them the wrong way would not go well for her under the circumstances. "I'm not working for anyone. I went there for a job interview. I would request you to talk to Mr. Singhal. He had fixed the meeting well in advance."

"Why did you detain Mr. Seth when he was entering the restaurant?"

"I didn't! I told you he came in my way. Listen, at least check my credentials with—"

The door of the cell opened, screeching ominously, and the inspector, who had made her life hell for the first two hours of the interrogation, entered the dusty room. The sub-inspector stood up deferentially and made way for him. Not meeting her eyes, the inspector glanced sheepishly at his team members and said, "I apologize for detaining you, Ms. Sinha. Here is your phone. You are free to go, but Mr. Kaul would like to have a word with you before you leave."

Esha wasn't surprised on hearing the name. She had reported to DIG Kaul for a brief period of time during her service. Though the delay was unexpected, she had been waiting for his intervention the moment she had given her credentials to the police.

The sub-inspector did not meet her eyes as she left the lock-up.

***

"**Looks innocent enough**... her foot got entangled in the chair and she fell. Her fall, kind of saved me..." Vikram replayed the grainy black and white CCTV footage of the incident for the third time in his suite at the Taj Mahal hotel. The video had been enlarged at some crucial places, distorting the resolution. "...though why she ran to the boundary wall is beyond me."

He squinted at the images and adjusted the laptop sitting on top of his notes on the study table for a better view. The cameras did not capture anything beyond the fence of the Golf Club, though the police had found an abandoned sniper rifle in the green-belt adjoining the club's boundary.

Baggah, hit by the first shot, was in the hospital undergoing surgery. He was critical, and the doctors were not very hopeful.

Nikhil studied the crime scene pictures left by the police ten minutes back. The dead chameleon cut precisely in two halves gave him goosebumps. What kind of a maniac could have done that? He shoved the pictures back in the yellow manila envelope and threw them on the coffee table.

"I have a bad feeling about this, Vikram. I've called Uday into this and I think you should go back to Mumbai immediately." Nikhil handed Vikram his drink from the room's well-stocked bar. The snacks trolley they had ordered an hour back stood near the table, forgotten in the flurry of phone calls from family, friends, and police officials.

"Not again! We have had this discussion a number of times, Nick. I'll go as scheduled, after the dinner meeting tomorrow. Have to tie up a few loose ends of the Myanmar deal. No crazy gun-toting person can make me hide in a cave. If I do, they win." Vikram paused the video when he didn't get a response from Nikhil and glanced back, craning his neck. Nikhil stood behind him, massaging his jaw, eyes intent on something above the screen. "Nick?"

"Hmm... I was just thinking..."

"What?"

"What if Baggah hadn't stood up?"

"He would have received the bullet on his head instead of the chest. He was being threatened for quite some time—"

"So are you. Remember the IB report on the Myanmar project you are investing in?"

"Hah... that's hogwash... rebels in Myanmar don't have enough funds to operate in their own country, leave aside planning an assassination attempt on me here in India." He lit a cigarette.

"Then why the second bullet?"

Vikram took a deep drag. In all probability, he was the target, but he didn't want to attach more importance to the incident in front of his family and Nick till the time the investigations revealed the entire picture. Adding to their worry and anxiety with unnecessary attention would not help anyone.

"I have no idea, Nick." He tapped the cigarette over the ashtray. "Let's wait for the detailed reports from Uday and the police. Tighten the security, I don't mind, but don't ask me to stop work. If I agree to all your precautions, I'll end up sitting inside a bunker room with three exits, playing Poker with you." He smiled to take out the sting that had crept into his tone.

Nikhil, as usual, indifferent to his requirement of striking the right balance between security and freedom, continued to stare at something outside the window. He was a loyal friend, a fierce bodyguard, and a dedicated chauffeur all rolled into one. Vikram could never thank God enough for his friendship, even if the man was a paranoid sonofabitch. He chuckled silently.

It had all started that winter years ago when he had met Nikhil on a treacherous Kangari Mountain trek in Ladakh. The guide had paired them for the duration of the trek. In addition to sharing the tent, they found themselves sharing many a thing as young men in their twenties. He had loved Nikhil's down-to-earth attitude, more so since the latter was completely oblivious to Vikram's status and family fame. That winter was the beginning of a lifelong friendship and a deep bond between them.

Seven days into the trek, when they were returning, Nikhil's rope broke. He slipped on the incline and toppled over. It was Vikram's quick reflexes that had saved him. Catching hold of Nikhil's jacket belt, Vikram had hauled him to safety by sheer willpower. In the process, Vikram had dislocated a shoulder and cracked a couple of ribs, but had earned Nikhil's priceless loyalty.

After that near meeting with God, Nikhil had become Vikram's devoted slave. He closed his private investigation agency and joined Vikram as his round-the-clock personal bodyguard-cum-chauffeur. Heading the security department of Seth Industries, he took care of the personal security for Vikram's mother, too. He was as dedicated as humanly possible, so much so that Vikram had to force him to take a break once in a while.

"Tighten the security. Yes—" Nikhil broke off as his cell phone rang and took the call. "Mahajan speaking... yes. Ah yes... okay... really? This is surprising. Yes, of course, I'd like to thank her personally. Thank you. And Mr. Kaul, I request you to keep the lid on Major Sinha's identity... er yes, thank you." He disconnected and looked at Vikram. "Your savior is a decorated ex-army officer. Major Esha Sinha, NSG trained black cat commando, one of the few ladies to have successfully completed the training and having five years of classified service under her belt. She has been given a clean chit. No wonder she assessed the situation so fast."

"No wonder..." Something clicked in Vikram's mind like a jigsaw puzzle falling in place—the posture, the alert, intelligent eyes, and the dash to the boundary fence.

"She had come there for an interview for some position in a security firm," Nikhil continued. "Though she has given her statement to the police, I wanted to hear a firsthand account of events from her point of view. I have asked Kaul to request her to meet us today, if that's possible. Would you like to be present?"

"Yes, of course." Vikram was surprised not just at his quick response, but also at the potent desire to see her again.

End of Bonus Read

Jugnu - The Firefly

Ashima's life is a long, tiresome struggle, until a tall, tattoo flaunting stranger registers in her guest house. Hoping against hope for a ray of sunshine in her life, unbridled attraction to a stranger is not what Ashima bargains for...

Zayd Abbas Rizvi, out on parole, wants to escape the suspicious eyes of the world and concentrate on rebuilding his future. He zeroes in on Kasauli, a small, quaint hill town.

Contrary to his expectations though, he is unable to find peace in the skirmish around the guest house, the antics of a three-year-old, and the deep, sad eyes of his mother. As he battles the demons of his past, falling in love is not in Zayd's plan...

Will Zayd and Ashima be able to forego their past and embrace their present, even when they know that if things went wrong, all they'll be left with is a broken heart and painful memories?

Jugnu on Amazon

Bewitched

The eternal dance of attraction, lust and love has been going on since time immemorial.

The divine apsara Menaka descends to Earth at Indra's behest to distract the sage Vishwamitra from the penance that would bring him unimaginable powers. Menaka succeeds in bewitching Vishwamitra, but her actions are destined to have dire consequences for both.

Eons later, their story is set to repeat itself.

Poorva has always played by society's rules and ideas of decorum. But what happens when her own loved ones betray her in the worst way imaginable? Does she still have to remain bound by their rules?

Rudra plays with power and people like they are pieces on a chessboard. He has no qualms about indulging his desires, be it money or women, but is determined not to be bound by either.

What happens when these two diametrically opposite souls are brought together by fate?

In the game of power, lust, greed and betrayal, some win and some lose. But are there any winners or losers in the game of love?

Like Menaka and Vishwamitra, are Poorva and Rudra too destined to see their story end in tragedy? Or will the divine power prevail?

Bewitched on Amazon